BlueBerried Muffins

A Black Cat Cafe Cozy Mystery Series

by Lyndsey Cole

CONTENTS

Chapter 1

Annie had to leave. Fast.

She grabbed her backpack and camera with one hand and her running shoes with the other as she dashed from the apartment. Frozen grass stabbed into her bare feet like pins and needles but she had more important things to worry about. Her feet would survive only if she did.

Her '96 Saab sat all alone on the side of the street in the early morning light and she promised something ridiculous like never eating chocolate again if it started up. With almost 300,000 miles on it, she never knew what would happen when she turned the key. But this time Sally purred like a kitten. Throwing her into first gear, she rolled away only wondering for a second if she was jumping from the fire into the frying pan.

Annie pulled onto the highway, heading east, home to Catfish Cove with half dread and half fear settling in the pit of her stomach. There was no way she could stay with Max with the problems he faced, especially after she heard the threatening message on the answering machine. She knew she had to leave before his drama caught up with her, too.

But then there was the unresolved mess she left behind two years ago when she threw her meager belongings into the car and fled from Catfish Cove.

Annie flipped her phone open and read, for the umpteenth time, the text JC sent. *Someone burned your aunt's café down. She's too proud to ask you for help.* Was this someone connected to Max's mess and this was a message for her? Whatever happened, she had to get home and try to make it right.

Annie rolled past the town of Catfish Cove, New Hampshire sign around eight that Monday night. There had been a population explosion since her last visit. Instead of 2,349, the sign said 2,350. Wow, maybe someone had a baby, she thought and chuckled. The lights twinkled in a few homes but everything else was closed down for the night. Not that there was much to close down—a gas station, a general store, the usual tourist shops and Leona's café, which by the sound of the bad news, was closed indefinitely.

She sat in her car, parked in front of JC's house, rallying some courage to knock on the door. JC was her oldest friend but would that get a little strained now that she was back in Catfish Cove, she wondered. When she left, she'd never even said goodbye. Time would tell.

The front porch light cut through the darkness after Annie knocked.

"Annie! I wondered if you would come back." JC studied her for a moment before smiling and pulling her inside, wrapping her in a bear hug. "Come on in. There's a lot to get caught up on." JC peaked around Annie toward the car. "Anyone else with you?"

"No."

JC raised an eyebrow but was smart enough not to dig any further. "Are you staying for a while?" she asked as she led Annie into her small living room and gestured toward the one comfy chair.

Annie sighed and settled back, sinking into the soft cushion. "We'll see how it goes. It's hard coming back and facing all the old history. Tell me how Aunt Leona is doing. Was the fire arson?"

JC moved papers and magazines off the wooden bench, grabbed a pillow and made herself as comfortable as possible. "Leona will be fine. She always bounces back and she'll be thrilled you returned, you know. She always asks me about you. Your mom does too." She shifted on the bench, adjusting the pillow. "Tyler hasn't determined the cause of the fire yet, but everyone thinks it's arson."

"How is Tyler?" Annie's face lit up until JC's clenched jaw caught her attention.

"He's head of the police department now. He's moving on finally, after you broke his heart." She pulled on a broken fingernail.

Annie nodded. "I didn't want to but I had to leave and there was no time to explain anything. I'll try to make it right."

"Listen, I need to get up early to get Dylan to school and get myself to the police station for work. Are you heading to your mom's house?"

Annie turned away. "I can't face her yet. Can I stay here tonight?"

"It won't be much but I'll dig out a sleeping bag and camping mat if you don't mind the floor."

Annie finally smiled a genuine smile at her friend. "That would be perfect. Thanks."

***

In the morning, Annie grabbed her camera and decided to walk to town. She closed the door of JC's tiny house and looked past the big house blocking her view of the lake. It was a short walk to downtown Catfish Cove at the edge of Heron Lake with a stunning view of the White Mountains in the distance. The morning air felt crisp for the beginning of April and her breath formed a little cloud as she exhaled. With her face behind her camera, Annie concentrated on the waves lapping on the shore and a few fishermen braving the cold morning.

"Annie? When did you come home?" A familiar voice made her heart thump in overtime. Turning, she saw a big smile on Tyler Johnson's face as he stared at her through the open window of his police cruiser. Two years, the uniform, and a new position as chief of police gave him a different appearance, more confident, she thought. And his shock of longer dirty blond hair gave him an air of mischievousness.

"I got to JC's house last night. What's the scoop on my aunt's café?"

He shrugged. "Haven't figured out anything concrete yet but we'll keep working on it. Your dad is helping too, even though he's retired from the fire department." He rubbed his chin. "Did JC tell you?"

"Tell me what?" Her eyebrows arched up.

Tyler blushed. "We've been dating for about a month."

"I'm glad to hear that." She dug the toe of her sneaker in the sand. "About when I left—"

Tyler cut her off. "No need to explain anything. You had a lot on your plate." His car started to roll away. "I imagine Leona should be here soon. See you around."

Annie watched as he drove off, thinking how hard it was coming back to all her unfinished business. She snapped a couple of photos and meandered the rest of the way through town. Not much had changed except for a new building on the water's edge that piqued her curiosity.

"Fancy running into you this fine crisp morning."

Annie whirled around. "Leona!" Annie smiled, happy to see her aunt standing behind her with open arms and a grin from ear to ear. "I've missed you. What happened to your café?"

Leona held her at arm's length. "New haircut? Shorter gives you a more mature appearance. Is that what you were going for?"

Annie laughed as she absentmindedly reached up and ran her fingers through her wavy strawberry blond hair. "I cut it myself. All that long hair was driving me crazy." Annie shook her head and the ends of her hair tickled her neck. "This is easier." She focused a steely stare at Leona. "Now, quit changing the subject and fill me in. JC told me the café burned down, but that's all I know."

Leona stared beyond Annie, out over the water. "That's about all I know too at this point. Tyler is still sorting through the rubble looking for clues. I think the fire might be a blessing in disguise though." She led Annie closer to the new building. "I'll get some insurance money and I'm moving into the new Cove's Corner building."

"That's what this is?" Annie asked, pointing to the cedar shingled structure.

"Yes. It's almost ready for opening day. There's a café and two other retail shops. Come on, I'll give you the grand tour." Leona steered Annie to the back where a large deck overlooked Heron Lake. "There's tables and umbrellas out here and my ice cream window over there to the left of the door. I'll show you the inside."

They entered through the French doors into a hallway with the café on the left and two shops on the right.

"See? It's all ready and waiting for me." She paused, watching Annie. "I was hoping you would come back and be part of this new venture with me. Like the old days, when you helped me at the Take It or Leave It Café."

Annie scanned the room, the wainscoting in light pine, the booths with red seats, lots of windows, and the view of the lake. The space was warm and cozy. A smile slowly spread across Annie's face and she nodded her head. "I would like that. When do you open?"

"Friday is the grand opening for the whole building. It's the start of the Catfish Cove Spring Celebration weekend."

"I forgot about that annual event. Smart planning, the town will be mobbed with people for all the activities and especially the fishing derby on Saturday. When I was little, my favorite memory is seeing all the tulips blooming around town. It was like magic, even though," Annie chuckled, "Now I know those tulips were all forced to bloom for the Spring Celebration."

"There will be more tulips than ever this year. The whole deck will be filled with planters of tulips. Besides that, I have three days to finish stocking the supplies and get ahead on some baking and soups that can be frozen. But we can talk about all that after you get settled in. I know about a cute little apartment, unless you'll be staying with your mother?"

Annie tensed at the mention of her mother, Leona's sister, Mia. "No, I'd rather be in a place of my own." She wasn't ready to face her mother yet.

As they linked arms to walk out, Annie stopped. "Did you hear that?" Her eyes searched the café for where the noise might have come from.

A scratching noise came from the cabinet under the cash register. "I hope this place isn't already infested with mice or I'll be shut down before I even have a chance to open." Leona pulled on the cabinet door and a tiny, completely black kitty peered up at them as if to say thanks, before jumping out and stretching.

Annie crouched down, stroking the kitty until the loudest purr she ever heard rewarded her attention. Looking up at her aunt, she asked, "Is he yours?"

"No, too many cats already live with me. I'll take him to the shelter."

Annie cradled the kitty in her arms. "I'll keep him. He'll be perfect company for me."

The sound of the door opening behind them made both Annie and Leona turn around.

Annie hissed through her clenched jaw. "What's he doing here?"

"That's not the greeting I expected when I found out you were back in town." He cocked his head and smirked at Annie. "As a matter of fact, I'm here because I own this building." He stared at the kitten in Annie's arms. "This is no place for animals, get that dirty cat out of here."

Chapter 2

Annie stared as her father walked out. She'd hoped he had changed after her two year absence, but seeing him made her realize he would always be blunt and rude. No warmth in his personality. "Why didn't you tell me he owned this place?"

Leona shrugged. "I wanted you to fall in love with my idea first or you wouldn't give it a chance. Besides, Roy doesn't control what we do and I don't expect him to even come around much. Still interested?" She cocked her head to one side and raised her eyebrows, waiting for a reply.

A big sigh escaped through Annie's lips. She held the kitten, her new responsibility. "I'm in, with the condition that I don't have anything to do with him. He's your problem. Understood?"

Leona stuck her hand out. "That works for me." Annie shook Leona's outstretched hand to seal the deal.

"And," Annie continued, still gripping Leona's hand, "you promise not to push me to do anything with my mother either. I'll work through that mess in my own time."

"You know me too well, but it's a deal. Now, let's take a look at that apartment."

Leona brought Annie to an apartment above a detached, three car garage, next to a luxurious waterfront estate. The apartment was small. One sunny open space for the kitchen, dining and living areas and a bedroom and bathroom. Already furnished. Annie stood in front of the window enjoying the view of the lake. "There's a lot I haven't missed about Catfish Cove, but I missed the lake every day I was gone." She turned around to face Leona. "This is perfect. You knew I would love this place, didn't you?"

Leona smiled. "The owner is a friend of mine and he's away most of the time so he likes to have someone living here." She paused before adding, "In exchange for rent."

"What? No rent? There must be a catch."

"No catch. You need to check the main house every day to make sure everything is in working order and call him if you find a problem. That's it. All the contact information is on this paper on the fridge. I vouched for you so he's aware that you'll be here."

"How could you be so sure I was coming back?" Annie's eyes narrowed into slits.

"You know me and I know you." She shrugged. "I had a hunch."

Annie let the wiggly kitty explore the room and smiled as he sniffed in every corner before jumping onto the blue couch, curling up for a nap. "Smokey says we'll take it." She laughed.

"Smokey? I like it. A reminder of why I had to move my business. He'll be our good luck charm."

"Speaking of names, what about the name for the café? Is it still Take It or Leave It? Like the one that burned down?"

"I wouldn't mind a change. You know, new place, new name. Do you have a suggestion?"

Annie glanced at the sleeping kitty. "How about Black Cat Café?"

"Yeah, clever ring to that," Leona said, nodding. "I'll call my handyman, Danny Davis, and check if he has time to make a new sign—The Black Cat Café, and underneath, Take It or Leave It." She motioned in an arc, imagining the sign. "Want to help me get some baking done?"

"Definitely, but first I need to get some food and kitty litter for Smokey."

Leona gestured in a mock bow. "To the market we go to get his highness set up."

***

The café was a clean slate for Annie as her mind swirled with ideas to make it unique. "Hey Leona, here's another idea. How about we build shelves along this back wall and fill them with books. The only rule being that people can take one but should leave one, too. Sort of a book rotation, a freebrary."

"Freebrary?

"Yeah, free plus library—Freebrary." Annie waited for Leona to absorb the idea.

Leona's face was scrunched up before it broke into a big smile. "I can picture it. Fantastic idea. If we pull the tables away from the wall a little, the shelves won't even take up much space. "She opened her laptop. "I'll post on my Facebook page that there is a home here for everyone's unwanted books." Her smile was huge. "That fire is the best thing that happened to me in a long time. You, Annie, are the breath of fresh air that I need and Catfish Cove will benefit too. Now, on to the food planning."

Annie sat at one of the counter stools next to Leona. The laptop was opened to a recipe file. "Here are my ideas in this file and my plan is to make an assortment of muffins, scones, sweet breads and bars ahead of time and we can freeze them. I'd prefer to always serve freshly made items but try to have extra stuff in the freezer for backup in case business is busier than we expect." She pointed to a multi-level glass case at the end of the L-shaped counter. "All the baked goods will be displayed there, with the coffee and tea selections on a cart at a right angle to the display case. I want to keep the mornings simple and mostly self-serve with the baked goods and beverages." She checked to see if Annie was following.

Annie added. "What about a few made-to-order items, like an egg and cheese sandwich or wrap?"

"That's a good idea. I don't want to start off with that this weekend, though. I'm planning to offer several types of granola and breakfast smoothies, but I don't see why we couldn't add a few simple grilled breakfast items once we get a good feel for business." Leona made a note on her menu. "The homemade granola and various fruit juices will be set up next to the beverages on another self-serve cart. The breakfast smoothies will be made to order."

"That sounds like a good selection for the mornings. Do you have any idea what the customer numbers will be?"

"This is a better location than where I was before. We're right on the water now, which is prime real estate and where everyone likes to be. I expect there will be a lot of tourists coming through for most of the year and they can help themselves and do take out if they want to keep moving or they can sit in here and enjoy the view. That's why simple is best. We'll be able to handle a lot more people if we don't have to prepare individual meals."

"What about lunch?"

Leona opened a new file for the lunch menu. "Lunch will be more labor intensive with made-to-order sandwiches, wraps and paninis. We'll precut and measure ingredients so customers don't need to wait too long after they order. And I want a variety of soups but we can make them ahead and freeze them." Leona leaned back and waited for Annie to process all the information.

"That sounds like a well thought out plan. What are we going to make first? My stomach is telling me to send something down before we get too busy," Annie said, hands on her rumbling stomach.

"I'll make strawberry-banana smoothies and an egg sandwich for us if you want to get started making the blueberry muffins. All the recipes are in this folder on my laptop." Leona opened the folder so Annie could easily find the recipe.

Annie hummed to herself as she pulled ingredients from the big refrigerator and the shelves. The whirr of the blender was soothing and the aroma of fried eggs and toast made her mouth water. When the food was ready, they both sat at the counter enjoying the quiet while they ate the delicious food.

"How's my mom?" Annie finally broke the silence.

"Well," Leona wiped her mouth and put her elbows on the counter. "She's not great. I think something died inside after you left."

"That's not fair. Don't try to make me feel guilty. It's her own fault that I left and you know it," Annie said angrily.

"I'm not blaming you, and it may be hard to forgive her, but sometimes it's harder to hang onto the anger. She was trying to protect you. My guess is that she realizes what a bad choice it was to keep information from you but she can't go back and do it over. Are you still searching for your birth mother?"

Annie nodded. "Max was helping and I thought he was getting closer, but then the lead disappeared into thin air. I'm still wondering if he found out more than he told me."

"Max, your boyfriend?" Leona put her hand on Annie's shoulder. "I know how hard it must be."

"No you don't. You can't imagine what I'm feeling." Annie quickly wiped a tear from the corner of her eye. "Let's get this finished for today so I can go back and check on Smokey."

"You go ahead if you want. I'll call Danny and check if he can stop by to get started on the shelves for the books. Get yourself settled into your apartment, I don't mind baking by myself for the rest of the day. See you tomorrow morning, bright and early?"

Annie swiveled the stool around and slid off. "Sure. Bright and early."

As Annie walked back to JC's house to get her car, she called JC to fill her in about the apartment and Annie's job working at the new café. JC was happy for Annie, and Annie had to wonder if that was because it meant she wouldn't be crashing on JC's floor again.

***

The early morning mist hung over Heron Lake like a warm down comforter when Annie walked to her window the next morning. She remembered, from living near the lake for most of her life, that the mist would break up, letting the sun dazzle off the water, and the sky would be bright blue by the time most people were up and about. A few early morning fisherman bobbed in their fishing boats, enjoying the peacefulness of the morning. She checked her phone, finding a missed call from Max from the night before.

"I'm not ready to talk to him yet," she told Smokey. The kitten rubbed against her leg and meowed before jumping onto the window sill and gazing outside. His tail hung down and twitched as his eyes followed something moving outside. There was a small deck and Annie decided she would hang a bird feeder on the railing so Smokey had something interesting to watch. "I'm heading to work now. See you later."

It was still early but Annie liked being up before the town woke up. The walk to Cove's Corner only took about twenty minutes and gave her time to think about what Leona had told her yesterday about her mother. Walking down the slight hill from her apartment nested on the edge of the lake into the center of Catfish Cove gave Annie the comfortable sentiment of returning to an old friend. She walked past the one gas station at the edge of town, the small general store, with newspapers already delivered and waiting outside the door, and a medley of touristy shops selling all manner of souvenirs and locally made crafts.

The new Cove's Corner building was on the best waterfront in town. The old tour company must have sold out to make room for the new structure, she decided. When Annie arrived at the French door leading inside to the café, she was surprised to find the door open. It is a safe town, so people probably forget to lock up all the time, she thought as she walked in. For some reason, goose bumps traveled up her arm. Something wasn't right. She got a pot of coffee going, poured herself a cup and walked to the booth closest to the window to watch the fishermen.

The sound of a shattering cup on the shiny oak floor broke the silence. Annie's hand flew to cover her mouth trying to keep the scream inside as she saw a body slumped in the corner of the booth.

Chapter 3

A slight touch on Annie's shoulder and the scream escaped. Every muscle in Annie's body tensed for flight as she whirled around with her hands up, clenched into fists.

"Sorry," the intruder said as he backed up a couple of steps with his palms raised and open, showing he had no weapon. "The door was open and I wanted to say hello. I didn't mean to frighten you."

Annie looked into deep blue eyes and a kind, but weathered and scruffy, face. His hair was pulled back in a ponytail, clean but scraggly. She quickly glanced over her shoulder to the body, double checking if it was still there and she hadn't imagined seeing it.

It was still there.

Turning her gaze back to the man standing silently in front of her, she followed his eyes, now staring at the body. All color had drained from his face as he steadied himself on the table.

"What happened?" He whispered.

Annie bent down to pick up the broken pieces of her mug, carried them to the trash, and got out two new mugs. "Would you like some coffee?" Not waiting for a reply, she poured the coffees and put them on the counter, away from the body. Feeling numb, she functioned on autopilot until she could make sense of what happened. If there was sense to be made.

He nodded as he talked into his phone, closed it, and joined her at the counter.

"I called the police." He held out his hand. "I guess we'll be neighbors here, my name is Jake. I'm in the shop across the hall, next to The Fabric Stash." Jake pointed to a sign she hadn't noticed yesterday, Clay Design.

"I'm Annie. I'm working here with Leonia," she told him halfheartedly, still distracted by the thought of the body. She walked back to the booth and looked at Max, slumped on the table.

Why did he come here? Was Annie in danger? A piece of paper sticking out of the back pocket of his jeans made her curious. A pink paper, not his color. As she pulled it out, she heard people walking in behind her so she stuffed it into the pocket of her jeans.

Leona rushed to Annie's side. "What happened? Are you okay?" She turned Annie around and searched her face before looking at the body.

Annie waved her hand toward the booth. "This is what I found when I got here. That's all I know."

Roy barged in, took in the scene, and bellowed to Leona. "What trouble did you get into now?"

Leona worked her jaw muscles into a frenzy. With a firm, strong voice, she said, "Calm down, Roy. This has nothing to do with me." She tilted her head and added, "Maybe you know what's going on?"

The two stared daggers at each other for what seemed like forever to Annie, but was probably only several seconds, before sirens broke the silence.

Annie stuck her hand in her pocket, rubbing her fingers on the paper from Max's pocket. "I need to go to the bathroom," she said to whoever was listening and went into the hallway to find the restroom.

As she pushed through the door, the automatic light filled the room with a harsh fluorescent glare. Annie leaned on the sink. Her body was suddenly too heavy for her legs to support. What was happening? With shaky hands, she pulled the pink paper from her pocket, unfolded it slowly and read the words written in Max's neat printing—*A. Don't trust anyone! M*.

The bathroom door flew open. "The police need to talk to you," Leona said to Annie's back. Annie could see Leona's reflection in the mirror as she carefully refolded the paper and slid it safely back into her pocket.

"I'll be right out," she answered, but the door had already slammed closed.

Annie sucked in a deep breath of air, letting it fill her lungs before exhaling. Max must have had information for Annie that he wanted to deliver in person. And now he was dead.

The café was buzzing with people when Annie walked back in. Tyler, in his uniform, tried to manage the chaos—giving instructions, ordering people where to wait and talking on his cell phone. When he saw Annie, his face softened and he motioned with his finger for her to come over. He nodded toward the counter stool as he finished his conversation on the phone.

"Quite a morning for you," he said with his head tilted. "Want a glass of water or anything before you tell me what happened?"

Annie shook her head. "I'm fine." She leaned on the counter with her hands folded under her chin.

Tyler waited for Annie to offer her story but she said nothing. Getting the ball rolling, he asked, "Was anyone here when you came in this morning?"

"I didn't see anyone."

"What time did you arrive?"

"Around seven, I guess. I walked from my apartment. The door was open and something didn't feel right, but I didn't see anyone." Annie swiveled to look at Tyler. "It wasn't until I walked to the window with my coffee. That's when I saw him." She quickly glanced at the booth where Max was still slumped over.

"You said something didn't feel right? What do you mean?" Tyler said quietly as he moved closer to the counter next to Annie's stool.

"I can't explain. Just that when I walked in, something wasn't right, like a chill in the air."

"Okay, anything else?"

"I know who he is." She turned and stared at Tyler.

Tyler's eyebrows shot up. "Max Parker. We found an ID in his wallet. Did you check in his wallet too?"

"No. I mean, I know him. He's my ex-boyfriend. I left his apartment yesterday morning to drive back here to Catfish Cove." She wiped a tear from the corner of her eye.

Tyler pulled a napkin from the holder on the counter and handed it to Annie. "Did he come with you?"

"No. I guess he followed me here."

Tyler leaned closer to Annie. "Was he stalking you? Are you in some kind of danger?"

Annie rested her forehead on one hand. "I don't know what's happening. I left because I thought Max might be in trouble and I didn't want to get sucked into his drama, but I didn't think it involved me. Not yet anyway."

She turned away as Max's body was carried out.

"If Max followed you here, maybe someone followed him and will be after you next. Be careful, Annie," Tyler said with concern in his voice. "Where are you staying?"

"Leona found me an apartment on the lake. I'll be fine."

"The Cobblestone Cottage by any chance?"

"Yeah," Annie said, surprised. "How did you guess?"

"Lucky guess." Tyler smiled. "Leona and Jason Hunter, the owner, have been friends for a while. Listen Annie, take care of yourself. I've got to get to these other people now."

Tyler walked to where Jake sat, jittering his foot and chewing on his thumbnail. Roy and Leona were arguing on the far side of the room. Roy grabbed Leona's arm but she pulled away, heading toward Annie.

On an impulse, Annie picked up her camera and clicked a few photos. She didn't know why, but when she looked at her photos, she could see a moment in time more clearly than in real life. It always helped her analyze a situation. She thought something might become more important or a clue might stand out when it was frozen in time.

Leona nudged her with an elbow. "Hey. Want to take a walk? Tyler said he's closing the café for the day so I thought you might like to do some sightseeing, have some fun before we get back to baking tomorrow." Leona's eyes moved behind Annie to the café entrance and her lip twitched up in the start of a grin. "Don't turn around now, but a real hunk is watching this drama. About six feet tall, dark, almost black eyes, probably late thirties."

"A little young for you, don't you think, Leona?"

"I've been called a cougar before, but if you want dibs, let me know." She lowered her voice. "He's coming over to us."

"Is one of you Annie Fisher?" a smooth deep voice asked.

Leona smiled her coy, flirty smile. "Why yes, my friend is Annie Fisher, and who might you be?"

A hand settled on Annie's shoulder. "Come with me, please. We need to talk."

Chapter 4

Annie twisted her body away, remembering the words on Max's note—don't trust anyone. "Who are you?"

"Detective Neil Jaffrey." He pulled his badge out and flicked it open for Annie to study.

Annie glanced toward Tyler, wondering if they were working together, and she saw a frown on his face but he didn't interfere. She nodded at the detective. "Alright, but I'm not leaving the café."

He cocked one eyebrow. "You seem nervous Ms. Fisher. What are you hiding?" He took her arm again and led her away from everyone else to a corner booth. "Sit there." He pointed to the left side and he slid into the right. He methodically took a pad and pen from his jacket pocket, placing it on the table between them as he continued to stare at Annie. "Are you acquainted with Max Parker?"

Annie looked away. "We met at an art show in Cooper, New York, where I lived."

"Are you an artist?" he asked, pointing his pen at her camera.

"I'm a photographer."

"And Max?"

"He owned the gallery in town."

"Was Max involved in something illegal?" Detective Jaffrey put his pen down and stared at Annie with his elbows on the table and his fingers intertwined in front of his chin.

Annie stared back into those dark eyes without flinching. "No." She slid to the outer edge of the booth getting ready to leave.

Detective Jaffrey held her arm. "Are you sure? How well did you know him?"

Annie fidgeted and looked away from his searching eyes. "How well do you know anyone?" she muttered more to herself. "I wasn't aware of anything."

He tucked his pad back into his pocket. "You can leave for now, but we aren't done." He lowered his voice so only she could hear him. "Be careful who you trust."

Annie blinked when she heard those words and a coldness clamped around her spine. "What?"

"Be careful who you trust. I have reason to believe Max was involved with some dangerous people and they may think he shared information with you."

She slid back into the seat. "I don't know anything. I left because I didn't feel safe and I thought I could come back here to get away from his mess. Max was a good guy, always trying to help new and promising artists. Everyone liked him." She glanced back toward the booth where he had been slumped over earlier. "At least everyone he introduced me to." She dropped her eyes until the wave of sadness passed.

"Okay, Ms. Fisher. Here's my card. He tucked it under her hand and his touch lingered. Call if you think of anything else you want to tell me. Anything," he repeated with emphasis. The dimple in his cheek when he smiled softened his stern look.

Annie slid from the booth, pulled her camera over her shoulder and searched the café for Leona. She noticed her father staring at her but he averted his gaze as soon as their eyes locked. Leona was talking to Tyler so she walked to the doorway and waited, frowning when Roy approached her.

"Your mother knows you're back in town. Are you going to show her some decency and stop by for a visit?"

"Decency? That's what I owe her? I'll visit when I'm ready."

"Listen, Annie, I'm sorry you were the first one here this morning to find the body." She flinched when he put his hand on her shoulder. "Did you see anyone or anything else besides the dead guy?"

"Like what?" she asked with her guard up. Her father wasn't nice to her unless he needed something from her.

"A weapon? Papers? Maybe he dropped something when he came in."

Her hand slid into her pocket to find strength from the paper she'd taken from Max's pocket and to remind herself of his warning. She couldn't let her guard down, not even with the people she thought loved her. "No. Nothing."

Leona took Annie's arm, rescuing her from Roy. "Let's go, Red. We need to make the most of today before work gets in the way."

Annie couldn't help but smile at her aunt. No one had called her Red since she left two years ago and she liked the nickname, when Leona said it. It reminded her of the special bond between the two of them. "Where are you taking me, Nani?"

"You know, your mother was furious when that name popped from your mouth before you said Mama. Don't forget to grab your camera. I have a special friend I want you to meet." Leona had a glint in her eye that made Annie suspicious of this adventure.

Leona drove them in her bright yellow convertible mustang. "You still don't have a shy bone in your body," Annie teased.

As they drove on Main Street through Catfish Cove, Annie willed her body to relax into the car seat. "There's nothing like coming home to realize how much you missed something," she said, more to herself than to Leona. "Hey, what's that shop? A tattoo parlor? Catfish Cove finally entered the twenty first century?"

Leona inched up the hem of her jeans above her brown leather ankle boots to reveal the top of an intricate tattoo. Annie's eyes popped. "What's the design?"

Leona shook her pants back down. "A mystery for another day. How about you and I get matching tats sometime?" Leona laughed out loud at Annie's horrified expression. "Still not into piercings or other body modifications?"

Annie shook her head. "No. I'm not quite there yet. So tell me more about this mystery man you're taking me to visit."

"Who said anything about a man?" Leona said as she swerved into the parking lot of the Second Chance Animal Shelter. "I volunteer here. Grab your camera and let's go. And close your mouth, Red, don't act so shocked."

As Leona and Annie opened the front door, dogs barked and howled. Cages filled with cats lined the front room, some curled up in soft beds, others climbing on cat trees. A gray haired woman put her papers down and turned her attention from her desk piled high with folders and smiled at Leona. "How nice to see you. You brought more help."

"Karen, this is my niece, Annie. She adopted a stray kitty we found at the café but I think she'll like to meet the dogs too. She's always been a dog person." Leona winked at Annie.

Karen nodded toward the swinging doors leading to the back room. "You know your way around. Baxter is already howling out back. He recognizes your voice."

Leona gestured for Annie to follow her through the door to the back where the kennels were located. Pandemonium broke out with the dogs jumping on the front of their cages to see who came in to visit. Leona stopped in front of a cage with a big golden dog. His feet reached chest high on the cage and his head tilted backwards as a happy howl came from his mouth. He took a few breaks to add in a couple of woofs.

"This is Baxter. I've been walking him every chance I get. I guess you could say we are kind of bonded to each other." Leona lifted the leash from a hook and carefully opened the door to hook it on Baxter's collar. "Do you want to walk someone too?"

"Of course. I'd like to walk them all. Heck, I'd take them all home if I could, you know that. Any suggestions?" Annie's eyes took in the long row of kennels filled with dogs, not having a clue how to choose just one.

"This is Roxy, a real sweetheart. I think she's a lab-pit mix, and . . ." Leona grinned at Annie ". . . she loves cats."

They went out the back door to a large fenced in field with Baxter and Roxy. "First, we'll walk around the perimeter before we let them off to have some freedom."

As they walked side by side with the dogs dancing on the leashes or stopping to sniff the bushes and pee, Leona asked Annie, "Why did you come back to Catfish Cove?"

Annie shrugged. "The guy at the café? He was why I left."

"What? That was Max?"

"Yeah. We were together for most of the last year. He was a decent guy but there always seemed to be something in the background that I couldn't put my finger on. The day I left, I heard a disturbing message on his answering machine and it wasn't the first one, but I promised myself it would be the last one. I had to get away but I think he followed me."

"What was the message?"

Annie hesitated before stopping and looking directly at Leona. "Your time is up."

"That's it? Your time is up?"

"That was it. I grabbed my backpack and left."

"Did you kill him, Red?"

Chapter 5

"No! I didn't know he was here until I found his body at the café." Annie was a little hurt that Leona would even ask her that question.

"Why did he follow you?"

Annie stopped walking and chewed on her lip. "I don't know. I think he wanted to tell me something."

"That you're in danger?"

"I don't know. Detective Jaffrey asked me if Max was involved in something illegal. Everyone liked Max, at least the people he introduced me to, and I never even considered that possibility until Jaffrey asked me."

Leona bent down and unclipped the two dogs who were thrilled to chase each other around the field. Baxter was about twice the size of Roxy, but Roxy was much more agile and ran circles around the big goofy golden retriever mix.

"What do you think about Baxter?" Leona asked with a smile on her face as she watched the dogs.

"Same strawberry blond hair color as you. You'd make a good couple. Are you thinking of adopting him?"

Her smile grew bigger. "How'd you guess?"

"Your smile says it all. What are you waiting for?"

"I have to wait a few more days to make sure his owner doesn't show up. If no one claims him, he's mine." She whistled and Baxter charged to her, barely stopping in time before knocking her over. Leona crouched down and Baxter licked her face from chin to forehead. "Ewww. No licking." She turned her head away, laughing, and he sat down leaning against her with his tongue hanging out the side of his mouth. Leona looked up at Annie as she clicked away with her camera. "It was love at first sight."

"It always is with you, isn't it?"

Leona pulled a tennis ball from her coat pocket and threw it for Baxter but Roxy got a hold of it first. She dashed away with Baxter in hot pursuit but she took a sharp turn and his back end slid sideways when he tried to catch her.

"Why don't you adopt both of them so Baxter has a playmate?" Annie said.

"Maybe." Leona whistled again and clipped the leashes on. "Time to go back inside. I'll try to come by again tomorrow. You're welcome anytime, too. Karen is too busy to walk the dogs like this, she depends on volunteers. She wouldn't mind if you photographed all the dogs for her website. A professional photo can make all the difference in finding a home."

"I'd like to do that. You know how animals have always been a big part of my life."

Leona and Annie found Karen still sitting at her desk shuffling through her mountain of folders. She smiled at them when they walked in. "Did the dogs enjoy their romp?"

"You know they did. And," Leona tilted her head toward Annie, "I recruited another volunteer for you. Annie is a photographer and she agreed to photograph the dogs and cats for your website."

A smile as big as her mountain of paperwork spread across her face. "That's the best news coming through this office all week. Oh, I almost forgot, someone stopped by yesterday asking directions to the Take It or Leave It Café. I don't know if he was looking for the old place or the new one so I gave him directions to both."

"Someone from out of town?" Leona asked.

"Yeah, New York plates on his beemer."

Annie felt a twitch start in her cheek muscle. "What did he look like?"

Karen put her head on one hand and thought for a minute. "Tall, skinny, dressed impeccably, like someone from the city. Why?"

Leona sat down in the only other chair in the room. "Annie's ex-boyfriend, Max, was found dead in the new café this morning. He was from New York. Do you think someone followed him here?" she asked, turning to Annie. "Does that description sound like anyone you met from Max's art gallery?"

"Maybe his partner, Vincent West. I didn't know him well, but I met him a couple of times."

"Why would he be looking for the Take It or Leave It Café?"

Annie rubbed the pink paper in her jean pocket. "He could have followed Max, thinking Max was following me. I suppose he could have researched my background and discovered Catfish Cove and the Take It or Leave It connected to my name online."

"You should tell Tyler about this," Karen said.

"Tell him what? That someone stopped here asking for directions? Not much unusual about that. I want to find out if the guy is Vincent or not before I start acting like a paranoid fool," Annie said. She took her camera off her shoulder and walked closer to Karen to show her the photos of Leona and Baxter.

Karen scrolled through the pictures. "These are amazing. If you can get shots like this for all the dogs, they will be adopted in no time."

"I'm happy to help you and the animals. I'll be working with Leona at the new café, so once we settle into a workable routine I'll make time for a photo shoot.

"Great. I'll see you on Friday for the opening. Can't wait for a smoothie and a muffin."

"I forgot to tell you. Annie came up with a new name. Now it's The Black Cat Café—Take It or Leave It."

"Awesome name." Karen nodded.

Back in the car, Leona revved up the engine of her mustang. "Let's make a quick stop at Cove's Corner and check what's going on. I can't imagine it will take too much time to finish up with their investigation. It would be helpful to be able to get back in to get some baking done instead of losing this whole day."

They pulled into a mostly empty parking lot. As they walked inside, the yellow tape was still across the café entrance. Leona pulled Annie into The Fabric Stash to see if Martha had any information. She had a nose for gossip and if anything was spinning around town she would be sure to know.

Martha was bent over her long arm quilting machine, humming to herself as she worked the pattern through the quilt. "Hi Martha," Leona yelled.

Martha straightened up, smiled and turned the machine off. "Leona! And is Annie Fisher with you? I haven't seen Annie for far too long. How are you, hon? Have you heard about the dreadful happenings right here in the café? Yes, I suppose you would know." She stopped talking to laugh at her silly question. "How about some tea? I always keep my electric kettle ready to go for my customers. You're in for a treat today, because, guess what? There are a couple of cinnamon buns left."

"Martha, take a breath of air and relax, okay?" Leona kidded her. Martha had a habit of rattling on so fast it was hard to keep up with her train of thought.

Martha pushed her gray hair out of her eyes and poured three cups of tea. "All the excitement around here today revved up my adrenalin and it's flowing like a Ferrari on a racetrack. And that handsome detective?" She put her hand over her heart. "If only I was twenty years younger I'd be killing someone so I could enjoy an interrogation from him. I think he said his name is Neil Jaffrey. One of you should check him out. I didn't notice a ring on his finger." She winked at Leona and Annie over her teacup as she took a sip.

Annie settled into a comfy chair with her tea. "It's nice to be back in Catfish Cove and I'm happy you remember me, Martha."

"Of course I remember you. You and Leona, you two could be sisters. I don't know how you both ended up with that beautiful strawberry blond hair and your mother has long dark hair. You are blessed with your mother's eyes though, Annie."

Annie nodded, realizing how well her mother kept the secret of her adoption from her and everyone else.

"What did you and that fine-looking detective chat about?" Leona asked.

"Oh, he didn't spend much time with me, I'm sorry to say. He was talking to Jake, next door in the Clay Design shop. He was in with Jake for a good hour. And someone else was in there, too. A tall, skinny guy, not from around here. He stood out like a sore thumb in this town, too metrosexual."

Leona spit her tea out when Martha used that word.

"What? Did I use it wrong? I try to keep up with these new terms, don't want to be left back in the twentieth century, you know. Full speed ahead is how I want to live my life."

Annie chuckled. "You used it right. Did you catch the guy's name?"

"No. Their voices were muffled and I couldn't understand what they were talking about." She leaned close to both women and whispered. "I certainly tried to eavesdrop but they closed the door, and when I put my glass up against the wall, I still couldn't make out a dang word clearly." She dabbed at the front of her blouse with a lacy cotton handkerchief where a tiny bit of tea had spilled. "Dang it. Another blouse with a stain. Pretty soon I'll be wearing a bib if I keep this up." She looked up at Annie. "I almost forgot, the metrosexual guy stopped in here and asked about you. I thought that was odd since I didn't even know you were back in town."

"What did you tell him?"

She chuckled. "I gave him a hard time. You know, he wasn't my type of guy, too smooth and he has those cold, mean eyes. He asked if I knew an Annie Fisher and I said, Sandy? I don't know any Sandy. He kept repeating himself louder and louder thinking I would eventually hear him correctly." She slapped her knee and roared with laughter. "He tried to stay friendly but I could see the frustration building behind his eyes as he clenched his jaw and said one last time, A-N-N-I-E. I shook my head and he left. You should have seen his face. I could barely keep from rolling on the floor in hysterics before he got out the door." Martha added, "Your father came in, too. He can be so charming when he wants something. Usually he doesn't even give me the time of day, unless, of course, he's stopping to collect the rent."

"What did he want?"

"Oh yeah, he wondered if I saw anyone hanging around the building yesterday. Anyone unfamiliar. I told him, in case you didn't notice, there are a lot of tourists coming through town, have been for the last seventy five years. So, yeah, there were unfamiliar people around yesterday. Geez, does he think I keep tabs on everyone coming through?" She stood and stretched. "And if I did, I wouldn't tell him anyway. Sorry Annie, but your father isn't one of my favorite people."

"No problem, Martha, he's not one of my favorites either." Annie rubbed her hand over the quilt Martha was working on. "We'd better let you get back to your quilt. These colors are beautiful. I like how you mixed the greens and blues with a hint of orange. What's the name of this pattern?"

"Thank you. It's a modified log cabin style. Choosing the colors is always the best part for me. Well, that and doing the final quilting ever since I got this long arm machine." She patted her big machine fondly. "I'm always surprised how the pieces and colors seem to come together with a mind of their own and perform a sort of material magic." She shook her head, suddenly lost in her thoughts of her quilts.

As Leona and Annie headed out the door, Martha remembered one more thing. "Annie, that guy said for me to tell you, if I saw you, he'd be back."

Chapter 6

"I don't like this. Who is that guy, Vincent, and what does he want with you?" Leona asked as they walked out of The Fabric Stash.

"He's Max's partner but I don't know why he's looking for me." Annie turned right toward Clay Design instead of left to the back exit. "What's the deal with Jake, the pottery guy? He came into the café right after I found the body and scared the bejesus out of me when he seemed to appear out of thin air. I don't know where he had been lurking but it was creepy."

"He's a bit of a mystery man. He's extremely talented, and I heard he sends some of his porcelain pieces to an art gallery. He's kind of a loner, keeps to himself. I think he lives in a cabin out in the boondocks at the end of a dirt road. Your father wanted him in here, thought he would bring in a lot of tourists. I don't think he had a shop before he opened up in Cove's Corner." Leona's lips twitched up into a conspiratorial grin. "Let's go in and have a friendly chat."

"Hey Jake, quite a day," Leona said as they walked into Clay Design and found Jake packing some pottery into bubble wrap.

He quickly slid his knife into the holster on his belt and closed the top of the box he was packing. "Annie, how are you doing? That was quite a shock for you this morning."

Annie nodded. "Yeah, that's an understatement since that was my ex-boyfriend slumped in the booth." She wiped a tear away with the back of her hand.

Jake stood up and placed his hand on her arm. "I didn't know. I thought he was just somebody in the wrong place at the wrong time."

"It must have been tough for you too. You weren't far behind me."

He glanced at his watch. "I'm in the middle of packing some of my pieces for shipment, and I'm desperate to make this deadline. How about we talk more about this tomorrow? Not that I can add any information. That detective grilled me for far too long for the meager information that I have." He nervously shifted from one foot to the other. "I was planning to close for the day and get this packing done." He gestured toward the pottery lined up on a table.

"Sure. See you tomorrow. We'll be here bright and early catching up with some baking for the busy weekend coming up. Losing today hasn't helped with our opening plans, that's for sure. Tomorrow will be a long, busy day," Leona said.

"Can't wait for all the delicious aromas from your café wafting through this building to tempt us. I'll certainly be a regular." He smiled warmly. "Between your food, my pottery and Martha's beautiful quilts, I expect the tourists to be flocking through."

"See you in the morning. Coffee on the house for my neighbors here at Cove's Corner." Leona linked arms with Annie and they walked out in step with each other. In the hallway, they raced each other to the door like a couple of kids.

Annie whispered in Leona's ear, "Did you see his knife? I don't even know how Max was killed. Do you think he was stabbed?"

"Try to weasel some info from your old fiancé, Tyler Johnson, now head of the police department, or that gorgeous detective. For now, I'm heading to the grocery store to stock up on supplies for our marathon day of cooking tomorrow. I don't want to run out of anything once we get in production mode for the big opening. Want me to drop you off at your apartment?"

"My apartment sounds, well, exactly what I'm ready for. I'll stretch out with Smokey and watch the waves for a while from that awesome picture window. All this drama is catching up to me."

***

Annie made a grown-up grilled cheese, chuckling at the memory of Max and the name he came up with for her combination of cheddar and Swiss cheese topped with sliced tomato and a slice of sweet onion, toasted to a crispy perfection on whole wheat bread. She sank into the soft cushion on the window seat with her legs stretched in front of her and Smokey happily purring on her lap. The first bite of the sandwich gushed cheese out the sides and slightly burned her tongue but she could never wait long enough for the sandwich to cool down. Small waves lapped along the shoreline and a few fishermen, bundled up, braved the spring breeze.

"What do you think about all this Smokey?"

Smokey twitched his tail and mewed.

"Too bad I'm not fluent in mews." Annie chuckled and continued her conversation with Smokey. "What I know so far is—don't trust anyone, which makes everything harder, for sure. Max followed me here to tell me that? Or something else? I keep wondering if he found a lead about my birth mother. Did Vincent follow Max to kill him? Or find me? Or both? Jake, the potter, wears a knife in a holster on his belt. I'm not sure coming back to Catfish Cove was the best idea I've had in a while, but here I am and," she pulled Smokey into her arms, burying her face in his soft fur, "at least you found me. I can trust you."

A banging on her door made her tense as icy shivers tingled up her spine. Smokey jumped down and scooted under the couch with only the tip of his tail showing as it twitched nervously.

Annie went to the door. Detective Neil Jaffrey, was standing on the other side of the window, smiling and holding a six pack of beer in one hand and a bottle of wine in the other.

"I don't know anyone in town so I hoped I could convince you to invite me in for a drink?" he asked through the glass.

Annie opened the door cautiously, Max's warning ringing in her ears. "Have you solved the murder already?"

"Not exactly, but a guy's got to take a break, right? Can I come in?"

Annie stepped aside as Detective Jaffrey walked inside, taking in the clean and cozy apartment. He went to the window and whistled as he gazed at the view. "Nice place. So, can I tempt you?" he asked, holding up his offerings and tilting his head, waiting for a reply.

Annie took in a deep breath then slowly exhaled. "Alright, Detective Jaffrey."

"Call me Neil."

"Okay, Neil, I'll have a beer. Do you want anything to eat? I just had a grown-up grilled cheese and I'd be happy to make one for you, too."

His eyebrows went up. "A grown-up grilled cheese? Now, there's no way I would dream of passing that up." His dimple appeared on his left cheek next to his wide smile. "I don't even dare ask what's in it, just surprise me."

Annie busied herself making the sandwich while Neil got comfy on the window seat with Smokey curled up on his lap. "Awesome view," he said, watching her instead of looking at the lake.

When the sandwich was ready, Neil handed a beer to Annie and raised his bottle to her. "Thanks for taking in a stray on this chilly evening, this smells wonderful." He took a bite and the cheese dripped down his chin. "Delicious. What's the story behind the name?" he asked as he wiped off the cheese with the sleeve of his flannel shirt.

Annie looked out the window, not answering right away. "Max made up that name. When his son would stay with us he always wanted grilled cheese for lunch but it had to be white bread with one of those processed slices of cheese. This concoction with the tomato and onion and two kinds of cheese was our joke."

Neil put the sandwich on his plate. "I'm sorry. I was hoping to avoid that subject and cheer you up a bit, but I guess all I did was put my foot in my mouth."

Annie shrugged and stared directly into Neil's eyes. "I need to find out what happened. Why he came here. Who did this to him."

"Of course. He was important to you. Can you tell me anything about his partner, Vincent West?"

Annie walked closer to the window, staring out, but at the same time, not focusing on anything outside. "Not really. I met him a couple of times but he traveled a lot, lining up artists to feature at the gallery. Why?"

"He's here and he's looking for you."

Chapter 7

"Me? Why?"

Neil shrugged but didn't take his eyes off Annie. She could sense him studying her every movement. "You tell me."

"Listen," she hissed. "If you're here to accuse me of something, spit it out. You came waltzing into my apartment hiding your agenda with some beer and wine. I came back to Catfish Cove because my aunt's café burned down and I want to help her. Whatever you think Max and Vincent were involved in—"

Neil held up his hands and cut her off. "I'm worried about you."

Annie sank onto the window seat, glad when Smokey abandoned Neil and jumped up and settled in her lap instead. It felt like a small battle had been won.

"I stopped by to make sure you're safe. I thought if I brought something, it would make my visit a little less intimidating." He stood up, carrying his plate and empty bottle to the counter next to the sink. "All I can tell you is I've been investigating Vincent and Max's art gallery for a month and it led me to Catfish Cove and to you. Somehow, you're involved whether you want to be or not, so be careful. Very careful. I told you that this morning and I mean it more now.

I'll be staying in town until this is resolved. You have my number. I don't want to find you knifed in the heart like Max." His dark eyes burned into her. "Don't be afraid to call."

"Max was killed with a knife?" She barely managed to find her voice to ask.

Neil stopped with his hand on the door. "Yes. Does that mean anything?"

"Jake, the potter, carries a knife in a holster on his belt. He hid it when Leona and I stopped by to talk to him."

"Yes. I saw that too. Like I said, be careful and call me anytime. Okay?"

Annie nodded and watched as Neil pulled the door closed when he left. Could she trust him, she wondered. No, not yet. Not until she knew more about why Vincent had followed her and Max to Catfish Cove. She listened to the ticking clock, marking off the seconds as she sat and did nothing. She pulled on her warm fleece jacket, left the comfort of her cozy apartment, and crossed her fingers, hoping her car would start.

As she drove, she thought of the one person who wouldn't lie to her, not again.

The door of an old colonial opened and Annie smiled into the face of the person she needed to trust.

"Hi Mom."

"Annie, I heard you were back in town." Mia wrapped her thin arms around her daughter and squeezed until Annie complained.

"You're crushing me."

Her mother held her at arm's length. "I like your new look." She tenderly pushed a few stray curls behind Annie's ear. "I can't remember ever seeing you with hair that didn't hang past your shoulders."

Nails clicking on the hardwood floor brought a smile to Annie's face and she bent down to hug Stella, the black lab she had missed for the past two years. "You're kind of gray around the muzzle."

"She's slowing down a bit, just like me." Mia pulled Annie inside. "Come and join me by the fireplace. Your dad is out somewhere so it's only me and Stella."

Annie walked around the living room, remembering all the familiar objects, all the memories stored in this house where she grew up. It felt good to be back inside, as long as she didn't let herself get swallowed up by the reason she left two years ago. Would she finally be able to forgive her mother?

"Do you want some tea? Or something else?" Mia asked.

"Tea sounds perfect. But something herbal, I don't want to be tossing and turning all night." Annie looked at all the photos from her childhood while she listened to her mother bustling in the kitchen. Leona said Mia was protecting Annie when she kept her adoption secret. Protecting her from what, she wondered.

Mia brought in a tray with two mugs of steaming peppermint tea and a dog bone for Stella. "Thank you for coming, Annie. I wish I had done everything differently, but—"

"I don't want to talk about that now, Mom. There's something more important and I need your help. You heard about the guy that was found dead at Leona's café?"

Mia nodded. "Your father filled me in. He said you were the one to find him?"

"Yeah. His name was Max, my ex-boyfriend. I found this in his pocket." Annie handed the pink paper to her mother and waited quietly while she read the note.

"A. Don't trust anyone! M," she read out loud. "What does this mean?"

"I'm not sure yet but I'm taking his warning to heart and the only person I know I can trust is you."

"Even after—?" Mia didn't finish her question.

"Yes. I don't like what you did but I think you acted with the best intentions. I understand now that you wouldn't hurt me on purpose."

"What about Leona?"

"For now, I'm not showing this to anyone else. Will you help me?"

"Of course."

Annie picked up the mug of tea, blowing on it before taking a sip. "Dad owns the new Cove's Corner building where Max was murdered. One of the tenants is Jake Wallace, a potter. Can you find out more about him for me? Without letting Dad get suspicious?"

"I can do that." Mia put her hand on Annie's arm. "Are you in any danger?"

"I don't know, but the detective thinks I might be. He told me he's been investigating Max's art gallery for the last month and it led him here to Max and me." She paused, not sure if she should tell her mother anything more but decided to be completely honest, hoping that pattern would be reciprocated by her mother in the future. "And, well, Max's partner followed us too and has been asking about me."

"What's the partner's name?"

"Vincent West."

Mia leaned forward. "Your father brought him here yesterday. I never heard the name before, but Roy said he met him while talking to Jake at his pottery shop."

Annie put her mug down. "Keep your ears open and call my cell if you find out anything interesting. Don't tell Dad you're helping me, or anyone else for that matter. Something smells rotten about all this and I don't want to draw attention to myself."

Mia hugged Annie. "I'll do anything to keep you safe. That's always been my goal." She looked into Annie's eyes and Annie saw her mother's love looking back at her.

Annie smiled to herself as she drove through Catfish Cove and everything was buttoned up for the night. Not much has changed here, she thought. Maybe this *is* where I belong.

It felt good to pull into Cobblestone Cottage. She sighed with the thought of curling up with Smokey for a good night sleep. Knowing Smokey was waiting turned the cottage into a home for her.

The beemer parked on the side of the road across from her apartment, completely escaped Annie's notice.

Soft, cool sheets and a purring kitten lulled Annie into a deep sleep minutes after her head hit the pillow.

***

The early morning sun brightened Annie's bedroom. She preferred to have the lake view than close the curtains and block out the sun even if it woke her before she wanted to get up.

Stretching as she sat up in bed, Smokey jumped down and mewed. "Morning to you, too. Are you ready for some breakfast?" It promised to be a long and busy day so she poured extra food into Smokey's bowl and refilled the water bowl with fresh water before she pulled on clean jeans and a t-shirt. Slinging her camera over her shoulder and with a bit of apprehension, she started her walk to the café, hoping this day wouldn't bring any more surprises like the day before.

The delicious aroma of coffee and freshly baked muffins made her mouth water as soon as she walked into Cove's Corner. Good, she thought, Leona must be here already.

Oldies were playing on the radio and Leona was holding a wooden spoon as a microphone and lip syncing to the music.

"How much coffee did you guzzle already?" Annie asked with a chuckle.

"Not enough to get through this day. Here, this one's for you." Leona put a mug on the counter and grabbed Annie's hand, twirling her in a circle as the song ended. "Okay. Back to work." She looped an apron around Annie's neck. "There's a pan of my blueberry muffins cooling if you want something to go with your coffee."

"The sweet aroma made my mouth water as soon as I walked inside. What time did you get here? It's barely seven o'clock." Annie sipped her coffee, looking around. "And what are all these boxes?"

Leona pulled five more pans of muffins from the big commercial oven. "That's your freebrary. All those books need to be organized on the new shelves today. Danny will be here sometime this morning to put up our new sign."

Annie stuffed the rest of the muffin in her mouth, freeing her hands to tie the apron around her waist. "What do you want me to do first?"

"The last batch of blueberry muffins is baking. We need at least 50 plain cupcakes for kids to decorate tomorrow during the Spring Celebration. I'll do that next. You can start making the chili—meat and veggie—and chicken noodle soup. The recipes are on my laptop."

Annie put the ground hamburger in the biggest pot she could find, browning the meat before adding crushed tomatoes, onions, kidney beans, peppers and corn. While everything simmered, she chopped the veggies for the batch of vegetarian chili—onion, garlic, sweet potato, green peppers, crushed tomato, corn, black beans and tofu in the second big pot. Once everything was cooking nicely, she added the chili powder, cayenne pepper and red pepper flakes.

"This is the place to be." Annie put her wooden spoon down and turned around to see the smiling face of Danny Davis. "Got any more coffee for a poor handyman?"

Leona slapped him on the back and set a cup of coffee on the counter. "Here you go. You're my savior, Danny. Nice job with the book shelves. How's the sign looking?"

"Come on out and take a look," he said with a sparkle in his eyes. "It's all done, so you can take it or leave it." He roared with laughter at his own joke and Leona and Annie rolled their eyes as they followed Danny into the hallway.

The oval sign leaned next to the door of the café. The background was stained with a warm, rich sunflower yellow with the silhouette of a black cat in the middle and Black Cat Café in black letters above the cat.

In smaller letters at the bottom was Leona's motto, Take It or Leave It. A thin lime green line framed the sign and matched the cat's eye.

"So, why did you change the name, Leona?"

"Annie found a black kitten inside on the day she arrived." Leona gazed quickly at Annie from the corner of her eyes and shrugged. " I guess we're both ready for some changes."

"I'll hang the sign as soon as I sample a couple of your muffins." He patted his stomach. "Got to keep this beast happy. By the way," he hung his head down, looking a little sheepish, "I fell asleep in your office two nights ago, after you left. Ya know, when I was building the bookshelves? Had a little too much to drink, I guess."

"You were here? What time?" Annie asked, shocked that Danny might have been in the café when Max was there.

"It was early morning by the time I woke up. Some guy gave me a hard time, wanted to get into the café."

"Was he wearing a flannel shirt?"

"I think so, red and black plaid. Why? Did you see him when you got here?"

Leona looked at Annie before replying. "It sounds like it was Max, the guy who was murdered. You heard about that, didn't you?"

"No," Danny said sheepishly. "I went home and slept off a hangover."

"What happened to your face Danny? Were you in a fight?" Annie kept her voice calm but dread settled in her stomach.

Chapter 8

Danny's hand went to his face. "Huh, I don't know. Must have fallen into something." He pulled his Red Sox baseball cap off, ran his fingers through his hair and looked from Annie to Leona. "I don't always remember what I do. Can I get those muffins now?"

Leona linked her arm through his and they went into the cafe. "Sure thing. I'll fix you up and you can get back to hanging the sign."

Annie glanced into Danny's open tool box and saw a long, pointed steel tool lying on top of his other assorted tools. She made a mental note to herself to ask Tyler or Detective Jaffrey if they found the murder weapon yet.

The timer for the last batch of muffins went off and Leona pulled those trays out of the oven. Annie hurried inside to give the two pots of chili a stir and turn the heat to low. They still had a ways to go before all the flavors were blended.

Danny sat at the counter washing the muffins down with his black coffee. Leona put all the muffins on the cooling rack, chatting with Danny about his work at the café. "What time did you finish up the bookshelves the other night? They are perfect."

"I went out to get a bite to eat and something to drink and got back around eight, I think. There were a couple of voices coming out of the pottery guy's shop."

"That's late for Jake to still be at his shop. Could you see who it was?"

"No, the door was closed. The voices were muffled, but someone inside sounded angry. I came in here and minded my own business, got lost in making the bookshelves. That happens to me when I do a project, helps me forget the demons from the war. That and the booze. I'm not proud of it, but sometimes the memories get so bad I have to drown out the fear." Danny looked up at Leona. "You understand, don't you?"

Leona patted his shaky hand. "Of course I do. So, when did you talk to the guy in the flannel shirt?"

Danny wiped his arm across his mouth to clean off the crumbs. "I finished the shelves and got comfy on the chair in your office. I must have passed out, but I don't know what time it was. I woke up before the sun came up. Everything was quiet and I decided I was sober enough to drive home. When I walked out, the guy grabbed my arm, said he wanted to wait and see if Annie showed up and would I let him in." Danny rubbed the sweat off his forehead. "Don't be mad at me, but I let him in. He said he had something real important to tell Annie. He acted kind of desperate."

"It's good of you to help a stranger." Leona glanced at Annie who listened intently. "Annie wants to find out what happened to him. She was the first one here in the morning and found him slumped over, dead in that booth." Leona pointed to the window booth, the seat with the best view of the lake.

"I wish I had more information to help you but I can't remember anything else. I'll go hang the sign now."

Annie waited until Danny left the café before she asked Leona, "Do you think he could have killed Max and not remember it?"

Leona stared out the window. "That crossed my mind too. When he came back from Iraq he was a mess. When he's sober he wouldn't hurt a fly, but when he's drunk? Who knows what goes on inside his head, and he doesn't remember those times."

"Uh oh," Annie said as Detective Jaffrey entered. She turned her back to him and whispered to Leona, "I saw something in Danny's toolbox that looked like it could be used as a weapon."

"Good morning, ladies. It smells like you're cooking up a storm in here. Anything for sale yet? Maybe a cup of coffee and one of those extra-large blueberry muffins?"

Leona winked at the handsome detective. "Well, since you asked so nicely, I'll be happy to fix you up. How do you take your coffee?"

"A little cream and sugar is fine." He reached into his back pocket and pulled out his wallet.

"Don't be silly. Put your money away. Today, coffee is on the house. Tomorrow we'll be open for business and you can pay then." She set a mug in front of him and a plate with a warm muffin.

"Thank you. Everything quiet this morning?" He turned his head to the sound of drilling from the hallway. "Well, quiet as in nothing unusual happening?"

Annie started to move the book boxes around, unpacking and placing the contents on the new shelves. "Should I do this in any particular order?"

"The sign says this is a café. What are you doing with all the books?"

Annie felt her face heat up slightly. She hoped people weren't going to think this was a dumb idea. "We're offering books for free with the request that if you take one, you leave one. A freebrary." She crossed her fingers hoping he would understand her new word.

A smile spread across his face. "What a great idea. Did you come up with that yourself?"

Annie saw Leona laughing as she kept an eye on the interaction. "I guess I did. You like it?"

"Yeah. It's brilliant. Can I make a suggestion?"

"Sure."

"Organize them alphabetically by author. Many people like to read all the books from one author, so you might as well make it easy for them to find what they like."

"I was thinking that too. I'll work on this for a little while, then get back to the food prep, okay Leona?"

"It all has to get done today before we leave. I don't want to open tomorrow with all those boxes of books in the way." She moved back to her prep area, wiping the counter and getting new ingredients out. "I'm starting on the cupcakes for the decorating booth tomorrow."

Danny came back into the café and set his tool box down at his feet. "I'm all done with the sign, Leona. Is there anything else you need me for today?"

"I think that's the last project. Give me the bill and I'll write you a check."

Danny slid an invoice across the counter.

Leona scanned the bill. "Are you kidding? You didn't charge enough."

"I feel guilty for letting that guy in the other night, so I took a little off the bill." He shuffled from one foot to the other.

Detective Jaffrey's face turned hard and serious. "What guy?"

Leona quickly introduced Danny to Detective Jaffrey.

"Um. The night before last. A guy in a flannel shirt. I never saw him around here before. I was finishing the shelves for Leona," Danny explained, obviously growing more and more nervous.

Detective Jaffrey stood up, leaning on the counter. "Mind if I take a look in your tool box?"

"Why would you want to do that?"

Detective Jaffrey stared at Danny, then down at the tool box with his eyebrows raised. "My dad's a carpenter. I like tools."

"I guess it's okay." Danny slid the box away from his feet and flipped the top open.

Detective Jaffrey bent down closer. "You take good care of your things. Nicely organized. Clean." He pointed to the tool Annie had noticed before. "When's the last time you used this awl?"

"Not too recently."

Detective Jaffrey used a napkin to carefully pick up the awl. Holding it, he inspected it closely. "This one wasn't cleaned like your other tools." He pointed to something dark on the sharp tip. "Mind if I keep this and find out what this is on here?"

"I always keep my tools clean. I can't even imagine what that is." Danny's eyes widened as he leaned close to get a better look. "Is it dried blood?"

Chapter 9

Detective Jaffrey put the awl in a plastic evidence bag. "What's the deal with your friend?" he asked Annie after Danny left the café.

Annie noticed his face had lost its tough edge. "I don't know much about him, what about you, Leona?"

"Danny is an open book kind of guy, a sweetheart, but the drinking is a problem for him." Leona shrugged. "The way I figure it, he left his tool box here while he worked so someone else could have used that awl and put it back when Danny wasn't around. Are you going to arrest him? I can't imagine any kind of motive."

The dimple formed on Detective Jaffrey's cheek. "No. Not yet. First, I need to confirm this is the murder weapon. And you have a good point about someone else having access to it. Unless there's a witness who saw him inside before Annie showed up he'll remain on the list with the rest of the suspects."

"You have a list? Who's on it?"

Detective Jaffrey laughed before finishing the last of his now cold coffee. "I can't share every detail with you. Thanks for the morning pick me up, I'd better let you two get back to work. I don't want to get on your bad side because I'm the reason you run out of food tomorrow for the big opening." He winked, looking more at Annie then at Leona, gave a two finger salute and headed for the door.

Leona fanned her face. "I get overheated just being near that guy. But my radar is sensing he's attracted to you, Red."

"You're so dramatic. You're overheated because you've been baking for several hours already and this place is turning into an oven. Let's open some windows and let some fresh air in. Hey, Tyler," Annie said. "Detective Jaffrey just left. You better check out what he found in Danny's tool box. It could be the murder weapon."

Tyler hurried out after the detective, offering Annie only a wave of thanks.

Leona already had ingredients out on the counter. "I'll make us a snack before we get going with the next project. How about a fruit smoothie? I want to make sure my mixture passes your taste test before we start offering it tomorrow."

Annie cranked open a few windows, letting the mid-morning breeze fill the café. "There are a lot of fishermen out on the lake already. I wonder if they might have seen anything the morning Max was killed," she said, more to herself than to Leona. The whir of the blender drowned out her words anyway.

"Here you go, one super duper fruitie tootie smoothie." Leona filled two tall glasses and handed one to Annie.

"Is that really the name?" Annie took a sip. "Ooh, this is yummy."

"My motto is, take it or leave it, which includes the names for my concoctions," she said with a fake pouty voice. "I suppose I could shorten the name to fruitie tootie smoothie, easier to fit on the menu board."

Annie took a big gulp. "This is delicious and just what I need to get me through the rest of the morning."

"Did I hear someone say something is delicious?" Jake's voice interrupted their chatter.

"Hey, Jake. Coffee or a fruitie tootie smoothie?" Leona asked.

Jake held both hands out, weighing his choices. "My body is craving some caffeine but the smoothie sounds much more satisfying. Fruitie tootie, huh? Clever name."

Leona pumped her fist in the air. "I was right, Annie, it's a catchy name."

"How about the smoothie now and the coffee to go?" Jake handed Leona a beautiful clay pot with a black cat painted on one side and the word 'tips' on the other. "I brought you a café warming gift."

Leona caressed the shiny, smooth glaze. "Thank you, Jake. This is perfect. If business takes off, I'd like to order mugs with this design."

"Just let me know when. By the way, attractive sign. Did Danny make it for you?"

"Yes, he finished up this morning as a matter of fact. He worked late the other night installing those shelves for me," Leona added, noticing a twitch next to Jake's eye.

Jake picked up his smoothie and walked over to the book shelves where Annie was working. "Books? Clever addition. Is there wifi in here too?"

"Of course. This café is definitely jumping into the modern times. With all the tourists coming through, I think wifi will be a big attraction to lure them to come in, sit, relax, eat, check their emails or swap a book."

Jake picked up the top book from one of the open boxes, turning it over in his hands. "Can I take this one? I love a good thriller."

"Sure, but the idea is, you need to leave one too— take one, leave one. You could bring one in another time," Annie told him. "Did you get all your pottery packed up?"

"Huh?" Jake raised his head from reading the back cover of the book. "Oh, yeah, I did. You didn't tell me you know Vincent."

"You didn't ask. You were kind of busy." Annie turned away, shelving more books. "I only met him once or twice."

"How did he get along with his partner, your ex-boyfriend?" Jake asked.

Annie whirled around to face Jake. "Why don't you tell me? You seem to be all cozy with Vincent."

Jake's normally pleasant face turned into a sneer. "A touchy subject? Vincent is looking for you, ya know. It seems as though his partner left something valuable with you."

Annie felt her mouth drop open. "I don't know what you're talking about. Is that what the three of you were arguing about the night before Max was killed?"

Jake's jaw clamped tight and the twitch next to his eye started to spasm. "Who told you that?"

Annie smiled. "Apparently, these walls have ears, Mr. Pottery Man." She turned back to the books, hoping he would leave. Leona offered him the coffee to go but Jake stomped out without replying.

"Geez, Annie, that's not any way to treat our neighbor here in the building."

"What? Did you hear what he said to me? Vincent is trouble, I can feel it, and the two of them, Vincent and Jake, are in on something together." Annie reached into her pocket, making a decision about trusting another person. "Take a look at this."

Leona read the pink paper. "What is this and where did you get it?" Her face drained of color.

Annie glanced over her shoulder to be sure there was no one else around. "I took it out of Max's pocket before the police came. I think he used this paper for a reason—it was mine and he knew the color would catch my eye. I'm sure he came here to tell me something but someone killed him before he found me. I think he was worried and wrote the note in case he didn't get a chance to talk to me."

Leona folded the note and returned it to Annie. "Did you show this to anyone else?"

Annie sucked in a deep breath, exhaling slowly. "I showed my mother."

Leona's eyebrows jumped up. "When?"

"I went to her house last night."

Annie saw the hurt in Leona's eyes that she wasn't the first to gain Annie's trust, but she knew better than to say anything. The relationship between Annie and Mia was as fragile as it was between the two sisters with Annie always stuck in the middle of the two women she loved more than anything.

"Okay then," Annie emptied another book box and crushed the cardboard for recycling. "We'll all get together and make a plan, try to figure this out before," she paused, "before anything else bad happens."

Leona stood at the counter as still as the water on a calm day. "Like what? I don't like the sound of where this is going, Annie."

"The fire? Max being murdered? Vincent following me and Max here? People arguing in Jake's shop the other night? The bloody awl in Danny's toolbox? What else do you think I'm talking about?"

"You think all this stuff is connected?"

Annie shrugged. "I think there's a good possibility everything is connected. Now, let's get this baking done, tomorrow will be here before we know it."

Leona turned the radio on to the oldies station to drown out the bad vibes in the café. "Baking and music. That's always a happy combination for me." She tried to sound like her cheerful self but Annie heard the fear catching in her words.

Chapter 10

Leona filled the last open space in the glass display case with a raspberry scone. Wiping her hands on her apron, she stepped back, sighed, and told Annie, "I'm beat, how about you?"

Annie poured the rest of the cooled chicken noodle soup into a container, slid it into the fridge next to the chili containers, and walked around to admire all the baked goods. "This selection is amazing— blueberry muffins, banana bread, pumpkin squares, raspberry scones, fruit tarts, cupcakes, and every variety of cookie I can imagine. Something for everyone. I'd say it's been a successful day and I feel pretty darn good."

"True, but if we get cleaned out tomorrow we'll need to restock for Saturday. So most likely it will be another long day."

"What more could you want for your grand opening? Scheduling your opening for this Spring Celebration weekend will get the cash register ringing nonstop."

"Are the chilis and soup in the fridge?"

Annie nodded. "Yup, and all the meat and veggies are prepared for the lunch time crush."

"I'll be in early to get the breakfast cart set up with granola, juices, coffee and tea. First customers at seven."

The café door opened and Martha came in carrying two packages wrapped in tissue paper. "I made an opening day gift for each of you." She handed one package to Leona and the other to Annie. "Go on, open it." She waited with her hands pressed together like an eager three year old.

They both unfolded beautiful aprons, lime green covered with black cats in every possible pose. A yellow pocket was sewn on at hip level with 'Take It or Leave It' machine embroidered with black thread.

Leona and Annie tied the aprons around their necks, modeling as if they were on a high fashion runway, laughing, and twirling their arms. "These aprons will be perfect over our black jeans and t-shirts," Leona remarked.

"Martha, this is too beautiful to wear. I don't want to get it dirty," Annie exclaimed.

"Don't be silly. They're washable, but I guess I could make a couple more so you can rotate."

Leona and Annie linked arms and did a little dance, kicking their legs up as they swiveled their hips. Leona pulled Martha into the lineup and the three of them made a conga line, one behind the other, circling around the tables and chairs, laughing and singing to the Beach Boys blasting on the radio.

"Thank you. These aprons are eye catching." Leona hugged Martha and kissed her on both cheeks. "You get free coffee and muffins for life. Was that your motivation all along?" Leona kidded.

"Of course, hon," she said with a wink of her eye. "But I might skip the muffins." Martha patted her ample stomach and cackled. "Trying to keep an eye on my weight. Now, I realize it's late and it's been a long day for both of you, filling this building with mouthwatering smells, but I can't wait another second. What's new with the handsome detective?"

A deep voice cut through the music and sucked the gaiety out of the air. "This is quite the party. Celebrating your newly inherited wealth, Annie Fisher?" The fun vanished with those words and every muscle in Annie's body tingled with fear. She turned around slowly to face the newcomer.

"Vincent West. And what brings you to our quaint little town of Catfish Cove?" She gauged his slicked back hair and immaculate designer suit. "You look like a fish out of water."

He sneered at Annie. "And you, my dear, left Cooper without even saying goodbye. What was your hurry?"

Annie let her anger give her strength. "Why don't you tell me? You're acting like you already know all the answers."

The main door of the building opened and slammed closed, the sound of footsteps echoing down the hallway. Roy burst through the café door, glaring at Vincent. "I told you to stay away from my daughter."

Vincent stared at Annie for a few more seconds before turning his gaze to Roy. "You don't call the shots, old man. I came here to get something back and nothing will get in my way. With Max out of the way, the only road block is standing here in front of me." He headed toward the door, knocking into Roy's arm as he brushed by.

Annie unclenched her hands, forcing herself to relax, before asking her father, "What was that all about?"

"Be careful Annie, this isn't some silly game. You're mixed up with these crooked art gallery owners."

"What crooked art gallery owners? Are you talking about Max and Vincent? Max wasn't crooked, but I wouldn't put anything past Vincent."

Roy shook his head. "Don't play cute and innocent with me. You know exactly what I'm talking about. I know what you've been up to these past two years. What I don't understand, is why you bothered to bring your drama back to Catfish Cove." He turned and walked out.

Martha pulled Annie into her soft embrace, running her hand over Annie's hair. "Hon, don't worry about what that decrepit old fool said. We'll help you. Right, Leona?"

"Right."

A third voice chimed in. "Count me in too." Annie, Leona and Martha turned to see Mia leaning in the doorway with her arms crossed and a Cheshire cat smile on her face. "I found some interesting information. Where can we talk?"

Leona went back to her big fridge, pulled out a container of chili and said, "Let's go, I have a plan."

The four women squeezed into Leona's mustang and they drove around a bit to be sure they weren't being followed. "I hate to act a little paranoid, but better safe than sorry." Leona checked her rear view mirror one last time, decided the coast was clear, and pulled into Annie's apartment.

Annie climbed out last. "No one will ever notice your bright yellow mustang parked here, will they?" she asked Leona with a half grin and one eyebrow cocked.

Leona remained quiet. "I do know what I'm doing. Get everyone inside, close the curtains and get me the keys to the main house so I can pull my car into the garage."

Once Leona was satisfied that no one was spying on them, she checked Annie's fridge for something to drink. "Glad your priorities are straight," she said as she held up the bottle of wine and four beers that Detective Jaffrey left the night before. "Did anyone remember to carry the chili inside?" She looked at the three faces staring blankly at her. "Alright, I'll bring it in."

Annie found four wine glasses, some boxes of assorted crackers and sliced the rest of her cheese. "We can start on this while we wait for the chili."

Leona stomped back inside but she wasn't alone. "Look who I found wandering around outside. Should we tie him up and torture him until he tells us his secrets?"

Martha fanned herself. "Oh, hon, that sounds like the most fun I could imagine participating in for quite some time. Can I go first? I know you three must think I'm over the hill, but I still have a few tricks up these sleeves. And, detective, we'll drop the formalities and call you Neil. That's such a nice name that your mother chose for you."

The dimple formed on Neil's cheek. "Wait a minute before anyone starts anything. I wasn't lurking, I was waiting for Annie to get home. There's no car outside. Did you all walk here?" He glanced from one to the other, pausing the longest when his eyes met Annie's.

Leona clapped her hands. "See, hiding the car in the garage worked. Now, let's get this chili warmed up." She picked up the last glass of wine.

Annie handed a beer to Neil. "I'm not sure if you've met everyone. That's my mom, Mia, sitting with my kitty, Martha from the Fabric Stash across from our café, and you know Leona."

He cracked his beer open and tipped the bottle to each person. "My pleasure to meet you. I don't want to intrude, but I have some information I wanted to share with Annie, then I'll be out of your hair."

Martha took Neil by the arm and pulled him to the couch. "Not so fast, hon. Sit here next to me so we can have a little chat. So, tell me something, hon, are you married?"

Neil's face went from pale to bright red before he could blink an eye. He took a long pull on his beer to hide his embarrassment, looking around for someone to help him out.

Martha continued, "Because Catfish Cove sure needs some new blood, especially some as handsome as yours. And I won't mention any names, but I happen to be an expert on these things and I could point you in the right direction for some good catches around here. I'd put myself on that list, but I might be just a tad too old for you. Maybe you have an older brother?" She patted his thigh. "Listen to me, rattling off and not giving you a chance to answer my question. Go ahead." Martha gazed at Neil with her hand resting high up on his thigh, giving him her full and undivided attention.

"Well, I, um, what was the question?" He tried to scooch over a little, away from Martha, but she had him blocked in between herself and the arm of the couch.

"Hon, are you married?"

"No, not at the moment?" He acted as if it might be a trick question with a right or wrong answer.

"Good." Martha rubbed his leg. "That's all I need to hear. Girls, any questions for our good-looking guest?"

Annie chuckled. "I do. Do you wish you had gone to your motel room instead of coming here?"

"Well, I wouldn't exactly say that. You girls seem like a nice friendly bunch and I don't think Leona was serious about the torture part. Right?"

Annie shrugged. "She's famous for her knot tying skills. Probably perfected that when she tied her sheets together to climb out her bedroom window as a teenager. Or so I've been told." Annie winked at her mom who was leaning back, enjoying herself.

The pot of chili started to bubble over and sizzle on the hot burner. Annie took it off the heat, stirred it and got out five bowls. "Everyone ready for my chili? You can be the guinea pigs before we have customers tomorrow paying for this."

Neil sat on the couch like a deer caught in headlights, not sure if he should stay or make a mad dash for the door.

"There's plenty for you too, Neil, so don't run away yet. Now, how about you tell us what important information you couldn't wait to share while this cools down."

Everyone sat around the table with their steaming bowls of chili and wine, staring at Neil.

"I got the report back from Tyler about the blood on the awl." He glanced at everyone around the table. "It doesn't match Max's blood but the handle has his fingerprints on it."

Silence filled the apartment.

Chapter 11

Annie's hand flew to cover her mouth. "Max must have been defending himself. Maybe he picked up the awl from Danny's tool box and managed to injure the murderer when they struggled."

Leona fist pumped the air. "So Danny is off the suspect list?"

"Not exactly." Neil frowned. "He was at the café, so all we know for sure is his awl isn't the weapon. We are still searching for the murder weapon and I'm confident it will show up sooner or later. The blood could be anyone's, perhaps not even connected at all to the murder."

Annie's face sagged. "Sounds like a dead end. How does the art gallery fit into all this? Vincent accused me today of having something valuable from Max, but I don't have a clue what he was talking about."

"I wish I had more information to give you. The art is what got me involved in the first place and I never imagined it would lead to a murder. If Vincent thinks you have something he wants or you know where it is, he will come after you. Watch out for him." Neil stuck his spoon into his bowl. "Think this is cool enough to eat yet? My mouth is watering."

Annie was happy when everyone at the table dug into the chili. "Mom, you've been kind of quiet. Everything okay?"

Mia nodded as she stole a glance at Neil. "I'm happy to be here with you. Your chili is the best I've ever had. Where did you learn to cook so well? I know you didn't learn from me."

Leona chuckled. "It's my secret recipe. Anyone could follow it and make mouthwatering chili but I guard it with my life. I don't want everyone to find out how easy chili is to make." She held up her knife, wielding it like a weapon in case anyone tried to force her to reveal her recipe.

Martha piped in. "Where's the beef?" She dug around in her bowl. "All I can find in here is a lot of vegetables and some chunks of white stuff."

"Welcome to vegetarian chili, Martha. Try it, you might be surprised and find out you like it even more than the meat version," Annie said.

"Yeah, but what's this white stuff?" She held up her spoon. "I'm not a big fan of eating something without knowing what it is."

"It's tofu. Don't worry, as far as I know, no one has ever died from eating tofu," Annie teased.

Martha slowly put the tip of the spoon in her mouth and bit off a small corner of the tofu chunk. She swallowed, smiled, and gave two thumbs up. "Tofu, huh? Not bad. Where has this been all my life?"

"Right in the grocery store next to the sprouts and other soy products. Glad you were brave enough to try it. Pretty daring of you," Leona teased.

Neil slid his chair back. "Thank you all for feeding me instead of the torture option. I'll get out of your way so you can talk about me behind my back." He winked at Martha as he carried his bowl to the sink and rinsed it. "Oh, and it was the first time eating tofu for me too."

"And? Was it torture?" Annie asked.

"Almost, I think I'll try the meat version tomorrow. If you had a dog, I would have snuck the tofu to him. Just kidding, loved the tofu." He patted Smokey on the way to the door. "See you tomorrow."

Annie sat back with a satisfied sigh. "That guy's kind of slick. I'm still trying to figure him out. What do you think, Leona?"

"Besides the drop dead gorgeous part? Well, actually, call me shallow, but I can't see beyond a handsome face."

"You're probably right." Annie stacked the empty bowls and rinsed everything. "Anyone want a refill?" She held up the wine bottle.

Three glasses were held toward Annie. "Not enough to keep," she said as she divided the wine between everyone. "Mom, I think it's your turn to tell us what you discovered," Annie said after everyone was comfortable on the various seating choices away from the table.

Mia finished her last sip of wine and cleared her throat. "I got curious why Roy brought that sleazy art dealer, Vincent, to our house the day before Max was killed. I didn't spend any time with him. He gave me the creeps so I poked around in Roy's desk today and found his journal. Roy is a creature of habit and has always been a little compulsive about keeping track of his daily schedule. Not in a lot of detail, but notes that must be reminders for him of what happened when." She looked at the others. "When Annie left two years ago, Roy hired a private investigator to find her."

"I can't believe the nerve and distrust. I didn't exactly disappear off the face of the earth, and besides, JC knew where I was. Who did he hire?" Annie asked with a scowl on her face.

Mia shrugged. "I couldn't find a name in the journal and I didn't find anything to indicate how he paid the guy."

"Okay, so he found me, then what? Did he keep stalking me?"

"Yes. From what I could find, he made weekly entries in the journal just saying update from the PI. Right up to the week before you came back here."

Annie stood up, pacing around the room. "I wonder if Max found out about this and tried to warn me not to trust anyone. What on earth was the PI finding out about me? It's not like I was leading a particularly exciting and mysterious life."

Mia said, "Maybe it wasn't you. It could have been the people around you, Max and Vincent. And the art gallery."

"Dad is part of that art mess?"

"I don't know. I wonder if finding you overlapped with discovering something else that he thought you were part of."

Annie faced Leona, Martha and her mother. "I trust all of you. Let's keep this information between us and see what else we can uncover. A lot of people will be in town this weekend. Keep your eyes and ears open, especially with that scum bag Vincent around. I'm afraid he'll be here until he finds what he came for. And since I'm his connection to Max, my guess is he'll be hanging around Cove's Corner. It would be helpful to find out what exactly it is he's after."

"We're with you, Annie, until we get to the bottom of this." Four empty glasses clinked together.

Leona drove Mia and Martha back to Cove's Corner to get their own cars. Annie cleaned up the dishes before cuddling with Smokey on the sofa. "What are your thoughts? Was Vincent in the café fighting with Max? Or Jake? Or Danny? I wish you could tell me what happened."

Smokey purred and twitched his tail.

Annie slowly got up from the couch. "This has been a long couple of days but I shouldn't procrastinate any longer. I'll be right back after I get the rest of my stuff out of the car."

Annie struggled back into her apartment with a half dozen framed photographs. "Look what I found, Smokey. I don't have a clue why these are in my car. Max took my photographs to the gallery for the show. Strange. I may as well hang them here. Is that okay with you?" Smokey always mewed when Annie talked to him, making her feel a little less crazy for bouncing her ideas off her cat.

She set each one around the room to decide which to hang since she only had room for a few. The opening at Max's art gallery was supposed to be everything about food so this project was outside her comfort zone with her photographs.

"I forgot about this blueberry muffin photo. I'll set this aside to take to the café." She left that photo near the door to bring to work. She decided to hang three in her apartment. One was apples, scarves and mittens, another was a watermelon cut in a fancy design and filled with fruit, the last one was a beautiful ceramic bowl filled with eggplant, artichokes and wooden spoons. "Max did a perfect job with the matting and framing. He had an eye for making the colors come alive."

After the photos were in place, Annie stepped back to admire her work. "My next project will be the shelter dogs and cats. I can't wait to get started with that one. Maybe Karen will let me dress the animals up a little with hats or sunglasses." Smokey yawned and walked away, giving Annie the distinct impression that he thought it was a silly idea. "Only if they don't mind, of course."

***

Annie's phone ring burst into her dream. At first the noise became part of her nightmare, a shrieking alarm that she desperately wanted to stop. As she drifted from sleep to foggy awareness and realized it was her phone, she answered, wondering who was calling before the sun was up.

"Annie. I need your help at the café. Someone broke in and dumped out all the chili. I'm coming to pick you up. Bring your camera."

Chapter 12

With that, Annie's adrenaline kicked in and pushed any hope of sleep far to the back burner. Glancing at the time—only four thirty—her brain registered it to be early enough to make more chili if Leona had all the needed ingredients.

Pulling on her black jeans and black t-shirt, she quickly poured food into Smokey's bowl, changed his water, gave a few quick pats to the kitty that purred happily to stay curled up sleeping, and headed for the door as the lights of Leona's car shone in the window when she turned in. Annie grabbed the blueberry muffin framed photo and her camera and ran out to Leona's car.

"What happened?"

"I can't even think about that now. I came in early to give myself plenty of time to get everything perfect, and now I just want to clean up and get another batch of chili going. What are you sticking in the back of my car?"

"A photograph I think will be perfect in the café. When I left New York I had some of my work ready to hang for a show about food at the art gallery. I had a lot of fun with the subject and this one has a black cat curled up around a plate of blueberry muffins."

"Huh, sounds interesting, but first we need to get back on track for today. I called Mia too. She should be waiting for us. I hope that's okay with you? You two are patching up your differences?"

"We skirted around the big issue, but I think we're getting closer. How about you? I don't want to be in the middle of your sisterly squabbles."

"You're right, not fair to you, and if you can work out something with your mom, I should be able to also. You know, Annie, we both just want what's best for you."

Leona swung into the parking lot with the only lights coming from the café—warm and inviting on the outside, but what disaster would Annie find inside? She grabbed her photo and camera and followed Leona, jogging to keep up.

Mia was already hard at work, mopping up the chili disaster. Annie snapped a few photos of the mess before putting her photo in the office to keep it out of the way until they finished cleaning and had time to find a spot to hang it.

Annie filled another bucket with water. "I'll help my mom with the mess, you can start on another batch of chili."

The clock ticked the seconds away as the three women worked furiously. Mopping the floor until it was shining as good as new, and cleaning where the chili splashed took Mia and Annie the better part of an hour. Finally, with the last bucket of dirty water dumped and the new chili simmering on the stove, they all sighed with relief.

"That wasn't so bad with everyone pitching in. Let's take a ten minute break for some coffee and a blueberry muffin before we make the final push before the doors open at seven," Leona said as she poured three cups of coffee and sank down into one of the booths. "Annie, bring your photograph out here so we can take a good look and figure out where to hang it."

As soon as Annie was out of earshot, Leona whispered to her sister. "We need to put the past behind us and get along for Annie's sake. She's counting on us now more than ever before."

Mia nodded. "It's way past time for that." She reached out and put her hand on Leona's. "We both love Annie. I don't know why I ever felt competition for her love, there's enough to go around."

"What are you two whispering about?" Annie saw their hands intertwined and smiled. "Never mind, none of my business." She held up the photograph. "What do you think?"

"Wow!" Leona exclaimed. "That's perfect for the café. A black kitty and my signature blueberry muffins. Quite the modern still life. You are extremely talented, Red."

Annie walked around the café holding the photograph up in different places and waiting for thumbs up or down from Leona and Mia. Finally, when she held it directly across from the door, they both smiled and gave the thumbs up sign.

"That's perfect. Everyone will see it when they come in, right next to the French doors with the view of the lake." Leona got up to hold it so Annie could step back and get a better perspective.

She nodded in agreement. "It looks like it was always meant for this spot. I'll tap in a picture hook, it will only take a minute."

As Annie straightened the frame on its new home, Roy walked in. "I hope you aren't putting nail holes in my new walls."

"Of course not," Annie replied without turning around. "This hangs here by magic."

"Very funny." He glared at Leona. "Are you ready to open at seven?"

"Right on the button. Would you like a cup of coffee? On the house?" she asked with a voice dripping with fake sweetness.

He glared at each woman before turning and leaving without the courtesy of a reply.

"What's up his butt?" Leona asked to no one in particular.

Mia answered, "He's been like this ever since Annie got back. Something is bothering him but he sure hasn't told me."

Detective Jaffrey showed up next. "Am I too early to get some coffee and granola?"

Leona checked the time on her watch. "Yup." Then she laughed. "Go ahead and help yourself, but don't tell anyone we're giving you preferential treatment."

The detective nodded toward Annie's photograph. "Great photo. Was it there yesterday?"

"I just put it up. We're definitely cutting close to the wire getting everything done."

"I like it." He tilted his head sideways. "I think it's hanging a little crooked."

"Darn, this wire needs to be adjusted. It keeps listing to one side." Annie brought the photo into the office where she could lay it down safely and check the wire on the back.

Leona finished setting up the breakfast cart with the granola, juices and milk. She checked to be sure the coffee pots were all set and the tea selection was varied. Smiling to herself, she felt the satisfaction of hard work paying off. Her goal was to make everything as self-serve as possible to cut down on labor for herself and Annie.

Detective Jaffrey helped himself at the granola cart and poured himself a big cup of coffee. As he slid into the booth across from Mia, his right arm bumped into the corner of the seat back and he winced in pain, almost dropping the coffee.

"Here, let me help you." Mia jumped up to take the coffee and granola so he could massage his arm. "Did you hurt yourself?"

He rubbed his arm before picking up his coffee. "Yeah, one of those stupid things that happen that's too embarrassing to talk about. It sounds so much better if you end up with an exciting story to go with an injury," he joked.

"Any leads with the investigation?" Mia asked.

He smiled his charming, dimpled smile. "Can't share those details, sorry." He watched Leona and Annie hustling around, with only minutes left before the café would open for the first day of business. "This café is full of charm with the shelves filled with books, and all the mouthwatering smells. I predict a big success." Draining his coffee and finishing the last of the granola, he wiped his mouth. "I'll get out of your hair before the rush starts."

No sooner than he uttered those words, the café door swung open and an older couple walked in. The woman sniffed the air. "Sure smells mighty delightful in here. Oh, look, sweetheart, that wall is covered with books. Why don't you go get us a couple of coffees and I'll browse."

The man stuck his cap in his back pocket and shuffled to the coffee cart, taking his time to study the choices before helping himself to two black hazelnut coffees. He brought them to a table and returned to the pastry case. "Don't mind if I try a couple of those fruit thingies and maybe two blueberry muffins."

Annie placed his choices on a plate and handed them over. "Enjoy. And tell your wife that the books are for trading—take one and leave one."

"Thank you. This is a cute little town you have here. Mind if we sit outside and enjoy the view?"

"Not at all."

He paid and walked out the French doors to the deck. His wife was lost at the book shelves, muttering to herself before she chose a mystery. "I have some paperbacks in my car. When we finish our coffee, I'll bring one in to replace this," she said, holding up her newly found treasure.

Annie elbowed Leona in the side. "I told you so. These books are a big hit."

Customers came in slowly for the first half hour, then it was like the floodgates opened. Mia manned the cash register, Annie kept the pastry display stocked and Leona chatted with customers while refilling the coffee and other beverages.

Both Martha and Jake came in for coffee before they opened their shops but it was too busy for any conversation. Jake acted a little brusque and Martha waved and said she'd come back when it quieted down.

By mid-morning, a lull gave Leona and Annie a window to get the lunch food organized. Fortunately, the new batch of chili was done and all the sandwich fixings were good to go.

"I'm going to work on fixing that photograph so it will hang properly," Annie told Leona.

Flipping the frame over, Annie examined the paper covering the back. One side bulged so she ripped up a corner of the backing to see if there was something weighing down that side. Annie gasped as she pulled the object out. "Leona, come take a look at this."

Chapter 13

Annie held up a bag. "This was hidden inside, between my photograph and the backing."

"Holy tamoly! Let's show this to Detective Jaffrey. This must be what he's been looking for," Leona shouted. "Was Max a drug dealer?"

Annie searched her memories for any indication that Max could be involved with the evidence she held in her hand. She tucked the bag into her apron pocket. "No. We aren't showing anyone. Yet. Just you, me, Mom and Martha. This still doesn't tell us who killed Max. It just tells us what that someone might be after and it makes more sense why Max, Vincent and Detective Jaffrey ended up in Catfish Cove right behind me. I still don't know why Max hid it behind my photos without telling me."

"Maybe someone else put it there, did you think of that?"

"No, but anything is possible."

"Where should we hide it?"

Annie was busy reattaching the backing on the frame of her photograph. "Let's ask Martha to make some kind of a pouch and she can hide it in her shop. No one will suspect her. I'm going to hang this up and let Mom and Martha know what's going on."

Customers were trickling in for the noon rush so Annie had to postpone her visit with Martha. Her hands were busy making paninis, wraps and sandwiches in a constant stream of requests. The chili and chicken noodle soup were on the self-serve cart where the granola had been for the morning. All in all, Leona's organization was working perfectly. Mia took the cupcakes out for the decorating booth on the deck for the kids. Without her help at the cash register, Leona and Annie had to jump around in double time to keep everyone served and happy.

Tyler, JC and her son, Dylan, arrived at the counter to order lunch. "This is the cutest café, Annie. Leona sure did get her act together quickly after the fire," JC said. "I would like a veggie wrap, Tyler wants a turkey and cheese panini and Dylan wants a roast beef wrap. Just roast beef, no cheese or tomatoes, lettuce is okay. We've been walking around town and Catfish Cove is swamped with tourists and the fishing derby isn't until tomorrow. That will bring in a ton more people," JC predicted while looking around the café. "Where'd all the books come from?"

"Like it? That's my brainstorm. A freebrary—take one and leave one." Annie pushed toothpicks into the wraps to hold them together and set them on the counter. "Here you go, three lunches. Do you want chips too?"

JC looked at Dylan who nodded his head vigorously.

"I'll take that as a yes." Annie chuckled as she added a large pile of chips to Dylan's plate.

Leona came around from the back and pulled Tyler off to the side. She told him about the chili disaster and that Annie had photos of the mess.

"You should have called me this morning."

"I know but I was in a panic to get everything cleaned up so we could get back on track to open on time. I'll tell Annie to show you the photos."

"Do you have any idea who would vandalize the café?" Tyler asked.

Leona shrugged. "The same person who burned down the old Take It or Leave It Café?"

Tyler nodded. "Maybe. Unfortunately, I haven't found anything yet to point to a perpetrator. Do you have surveillance cameras here?"

"Roy had them installed but they aren't functional yet."

"That's too bad. It would help a lot if we had images from those cameras. You and Annie be extra careful." Tyler glanced around the café. "I've got some new leads on Max Parker's murder, but it's going slower than I would like. I'll be sure to check out Annie's photos later when she has some free time."

Annie smiled as her friend, JC, and Dylan walked out to the cupcake decorating booth. She had to admit to herself that JC and Tyler were a good match and Tyler would make a great male role model for Dylan.

A sneering voice rang in her ear, distracting her from her thoughts. "I've seen that photograph before. It's supposed to be hanging in my art gallery for the Food for Thought show."

Annie turned around and looked at Vincent, balling her fists at her side. Every time she saw him her blood started to boil. "Unfortunately, I had to withdraw my entries." The words flopped out of her mouth with the hopes of somehow protecting Max if he was involved with the drugs she found.

"And why was that? Hiding something behind the photographs?"

"What are you talking about? That's the most ridiculous statement I've heard." She turned and walked away so her face didn't give her shock away.

"I'll find it, Annie. Max knew he'd never get away. His high and mighty attitude, always helping those starving artists . . . that never brought money into the gallery."

Annie walked back and stopped mere inches from Vincent's face. "Is that why you killed him? You two fought right here in the café and he stabbed you. Maybe it's your blood on the awl the detective found," she hissed so only he could hear her words. Her lips curled at the edges as she watched the color drain from Vincent's face. "I plan on finding Max's killer. It's the least I can do for him." She kept her eyes boring straight into Vincent's dark pupils. "That's a promise."

Vincent retreated from the café and walked across the hall into Clay Design.

Something's fishy with that relationship, Annie thought. She wondered if Jake was involved with hiding and shipping drugs too.

Customers flooding into the café made Annie rush back behind the counter. It was all she could do to make sandwiches fast enough and keep everyone moving through. Change and bills were stuffed into the tip bowl and she overheard many tourists commenting on the café and how good the food tasted. She chuckled every time someone pulled a book from the freebrary like they found the best treasure of all.

Three o'clock arrived before Leona or Annie even had a chance for a bite of lunch. The chili pot was scraped clean, the pastry case wasn't empty but had been picked over and most of the sandwich fixings were gone.

Mia came back in and offered to help in any way needed. "Let's keep the ice cream window open," Leona suggested. "If you can handle that, Mia, Annie and I will restock for tomorrow. First, let's take a breather and refuel ourselves so we don't crash and burn."

"Is there any food left for us?" Annie asked, pushing a few stray red curls behind her ear. "How about I whip up three Chubby Chickpea sandwiches?"

"With a name like that, it has to taste delicious." Mia said as she slid onto a stool at the counter.

Annie laughed. "Max's son visited us every other weekend. He had a knack for putting words together." Annie got busy slicing wheat bread, roughly mashing the chickpeas and adding scallions, carrots, hummus, lemon juice, garlic and mustard. "Here you go, ladies. I hope you enjoy my creation."

They ate without conversation until the last crumb was cleaned from their plates. "Annie, that was amazing. I think we should add it to our lunch menu," Leona said, obviously thinking the chickpea sandwich tasted delicious.

"It's easy enough to make a big batch and it could be served as a salad, sandwich or wrap."

Leona was busy making a shopping list. "I'll run to the store and get all the stuff we'll need. Meet back here in an hour? Can you manage the window alone, Mia?"

"I'll be fine." She said as she hurried to the ice cream window to help a family.

Annie patted the bag of drugs in her apron pocket, checking that it was still safe. This would be the perfect chance to take it to Martha's shop, she thought. She untied the apron from her waist, folded it, and tucked it under her arm. "I'm going to check on my kitty. He's spent way too much time alone. Do you want any more photographs to hang in the café?"

Both Leona and Mia answered at the same time. "Of course!"

On her way out of Cove's Corner, she popped into the empty-of-customers Fabric Stash. "Busy today?" she asked Martha.

"Plenty of people are coming through and browsing but not much is selling. How about the café?"

"Busy. We'll be spending the rest of the afternoon baking for tomorrow's rush which, I'm guessing, will be bigger than today, being Saturday and all." Annie leaned close to Martha's ear and continued, "I found this hidden behind my photograph." She pulled the bag from her apron pocket letting Martha get a peak of what she had before leaving the apron on Martha's sewing table. "I think it's what Vincent is after. Can you make a cover and keep it safe somewhere in here? I'll explain more later. Just don't let anyone know it's here."

One eyebrow went up. "Sounds mysterious. Of course I will." Martha rubbed her hands together. "Nothing better than some excitement for this old lady." She sat at her sewing machine with a piece of dark gray fabric, sewing a small square cover as Annie left.

If she walked briskly, Annie could get back to her apartment in fifteen minutes, visit with Smokey for a bit and be back before the hour was up. The walk gave Annie a chance to clear her mind of the hectic morning and get her thoughts back to the mystery of Max's murder. He had been insistent on matting and framing her photographs. But it didn't explain anything about the bag of drugs, only that Detective Jaffrey said the gallery was involved in something illegal and Vincent followed Max to Catfish Cove. Someone else could have put the drugs inside the framed photographs. She refused to believe Max was involved. She decided he must have discovered what

Vincent was doing and he needed to warn Annie and get the drugs back.

Annie opened the door to her apartment, smiling at her luck in having this place to live. Smokey rubbed against her legs, mewing and begging for attention. Annie picked up the kitty, cradling him and stroking his soft fur.

As she walked across the room, her foot slipped and she landed on her butt with Smokey clutched to her chest. She let out a gasp. All of her photographs were torn from the frames and they littered the floor of her once tidy living room.

Chapter 14

Smokey mewed loudly. Annie picked herself off the floor, surveying the mess. Her photos were scattered around the room, undamaged but torn from the frames. The sound of the door hinge squeaking made Annie jump and reach for anything that could be used as a weapon.

She raised her arm with one of the frames held above her head as she looked into the dark eyes of the most handsome man she had ever seen.

He quickly put his hands up in a nonthreatening manner. "I hate to tell you this, but the frame you're holding isn't the best protection from an intruder." His mouth twitched as he worked unsuccessfully to suppress a smile.

Annie lowered the frame. "Do you make it a habit of walking in without an invitation?"

He took the frame from Annie and leaned it on the wall. Waving his hand over the mess on the floor, he said, "It appears you won the battle with these photographs. Did they attack you when you came in?"

Anger started to build in the pit of her stomach. Who was this tall, self-controlled man making fun of her, she wondered. "You didn't answer my question about walking in uninvited."

He stared out the window at the view of the lake. "I haven't seen the lake from this view since I built this garage apartment."

The meaning of his words slammed into Annie's brain and she felt her face burn with embarrassment. "Jason Hunter?"

"Guilty as charged. No, I don't normally enter uninvited but I heard a crash as I got to your door. It was cracked open and I wanted to see what was going on in my apartment." He extended his hand. "You must be Leona's niece, Annie. Pleased to meet you." His eyes took Annie in from her strawberry blonde hair down to her comfortable sneakers. "You look a lot like Leona, only more beautiful."

Annie saw a twinkle in his eyes. The heat from Annie's face traveled down her neck and she felt her heart do a little flip flop. Was he still making fun of her? She couldn't figure him out.

Jason bent over to pick up the photographs scattered around the floor. He held the first one up, examining it closely. "Interesting. A face created from bananas. Is it a self-portrait?"

She grabbed the photograph and picked up the others, piling them neatly on the table. "These were for a show called Food for Thought, but they didn't make it to the art gallery."

Jason looked through the rest of the photos. "You are extremely talented. These should be hanging somewhere."

"Someone didn't think so," she said as she gathered up the mat boards and frames.

Jason gently held Annie's arm. "You didn't do this in a fit of rage? Apparently, I stupidly jumped to the wrong conclusion."

Annie shook her head. "No."

"Who? Why?" Jason asked as he stared at Annie, searching her face.

Someone was looking for something, she thought to herself, but didn't want to say to this person she'd just met. Max's words echoed in her brain, *don't trust anyone*. Instead of answering, she stared back trying to hide her true feelings of fear and anger and willed the tears welling in her eyes not to spill over.

Jason nodded. "Okay then, you can tell me when you're ready." He leaned over and picked up Smokey. "Who's this guy? I never told Leona you could have a roommate." His eyes twinkled again, replacing the stare piercing into her thoughts.

"This is Smokey. He's a bit shy, but once you're gone he'll tell me all about who came in and destroyed my work." She hoped he got the hint that she wanted him to leave, but in case he didn't, she made a big show of checking the time on her watch. "I guess Smokey's story will have to wait, since it's time for me to get back to the café."

"Great. I'll give you a ride. I was heading in that direction anyway."

Annie didn't want to be rude to her landlord, and she was running late, so she reluctantly agreed to take the ride.

Jason held the door open for Annie but after they walked out she made an excuse to go back in for a forgotten item. She preferred to walk behind Jason and get a better view of him instead of the other way around.

What was it about this guy, she wondered. He exuded confidence in a casual kind of style. He was taller than Annie, but not over six feet she estimated. His dark hair was a little too neat for her liking. His clothes appeared to be custom made for his perfectly proportioned muscular body. He had a slight limp that she wouldn't have noticed if she wasn't studying him so carefully. "So, Jason, what brings you to Catfish Cove?"

He turned around as he opened the passenger door of his SUV, waiting for Annie to climb in. "I like to be here for the beginning of fishing season." He winked at Annie. "And I thought it would be a smart idea to meet the person living in my apartment. I trust Leona only so far, since she has been known to make some poor choices. I wanted to make sure for myself that she didn't install a serial killer or decide to hide a terrorist right here under my nose."

Annie decided to play his game. "How can you be sure I'm not hiding some secret identity from you?"

"I'll just need to get to know you better to be sure. After all, you do have keys to my house. And you have a cat that appears to be a spy, which does make me suspicious of your background."

He turned in and parked in the last open spot at the Cove's Corner lot. "This is a busy weekend."

Annie hopped out. "Thanks for the ride." She wasn't completely disappointed to see Jason get out too.

"I'm fine walking in by myself."

"One can never be too careful." He took Annie by the arm and guided her through the doorway. "Something smells good in here. Leona certainly knows how to cook up a storm."

Martha peered out of her shop as Annie and Jason walked by. "Annie, can I talk to you for a minute?"

Pulling away from Jason, she walked into The Fabric Stash and Jason continued to the café. "Thanks for rescuing me from that guy."

"Are you kidding? He doesn't look like someone you need to be rescued from. Just the opposite. I'd let him to do all the rescuing possible. Who is he?"

"My landlord, Jason Hunter."

"*That's* Jason Hunter? I haven't seen him around town for, well, I can't even remember when he was here last," Martha said as she raised her eyebrows suggestively. "What's he doing here?"

"He said he likes to come for fishing season." Glancing around to be sure they were alone, Annie asked, "Is everything safe?"

"Safe and sound, but someone interesting came in and poked around."

"Who?"

"That varmint, Vincent. That has a nice ring, doesn't it? Vinny the varmint; fits his personality too. He certainly wasn't looking for any quilting fabric, but don't worry, there's no way he'd find your item here."

"When I went home, all my other photographs were torn apart and scattered around. That's when Jason walked in. I'm glad I found this one before anyone else did."

"Were there more?"

"I don't know. I found the one you're hiding by accident. My guess is, whoever is after it won't leave until they find everything they're looking for."

"Looking for what?" a deep voice asked.

Martha's eyes moved behind Annie and smiled at Detective Jaffrey, who appeared from thin air. "Just some special fabric with cats on it. I'm making aprons for the café like this one." She handed the apron back to Annie. "I didn't want anyone to buy it out from under me. Ya know, if you have a special someone in your life, I could help you find a unique gift for her. Or even make something if you're going to be in town for a few more days."

Annie chuckled. She loved how Martha could get information in such a casual manner. Martha certainly was an asset, along with Leona and Mia, in figuring out what happened to Max.

Who was Max referring to when he left that cryptic note about not trusting anyone, she wondered. Vincent was at the top of Annie's mental list but there were others too—Jake, Danny, Detective Jaffrey, and now Jason.

A crash from across the hallway drowned out the thoughts in her head. The detective was the first out the door, entering the café in just a few strides of his long legs. Annie was hot on his heels.

Mia was staring at the floor near the freebrary, staring at something shiny on the floor.

Chapter 15

"Don't touch anything," Detective Jaffrey commanded as he carefully pulled on plastic gloves and picked up a knife. The blade was broken off about an inch or so from the tip. "How did this get here?" He looked at Mia and Leona. Jason was standing off to one side watching the ordeal.

Mia shrugged. "I was straightening the books and it slid off the shelf."

Annie inched closer to inspect it better. "That is just like the knife I saw Jake using when he was packing his pottery."

Detective Jaffrey dropped the knife into an evidence bag. "I'll get it checked to find out if this is the murder weapon. Can I grab a coffee for the road?"

Leona, all starry eyed, walked to the coffee cart. "I'll fix it for you. Cream and sugar, right?" she asked, fluttering her eyelids.

Mia headed back to the ice cream window where a family of five was lined up. The three young kids were hopping up and down, chanting, "Ice cream please, ice cream please!"

Detective Jaffrey left with his coffee and a wink for Leona. What a flirt he is, thought Annie. He knows how to play the women.

The timer on the oven got Leona hustling to take out five trays of blueberry muffins and she slid in five more trays of raspberry scones. "Annie, can you make more chili and your Chubby Chickpea Salad mixture? I got all the ingredients for a double batch of each. Roy wants me to stay open tomorrow afternoon with the ice cream window and for customers to come in for the drink cart and pastries, so I'm not expecting much sleep tonight."

"Is he going to help serve?" Annie asked with disgust dripping from her voice.

"Ha! Would you want him to?"

Jason, who had been sitting quietly in a booth by himself, stood up. "I'll help. I like to see all the tourists coming through town."

Annie tensed, and at the same time felt her face flush. "What's your specialty in the kitchen? Making a mess?"

He rewarded her insult with a charming shine in his eye. "You pegged me accurately; I'm pretty incompetent in the kitchen but I think I can keep the coffee pots going. Of course, if you don't need an extra set of hands . . ."

"Of course we'll take your help," Leona shouted from behind the counter as she gave a look to Annie that said, are you crazy? "I want to make a big splash this weekend and I'm sure I can find something for even the most incompetent person to do."

"Are you calling me incompetent, Leona?" Jason said with his arms crossed over his chest and his lips squished together in a fake frown.

"Of course not. You know what I mean. Now, make yourself useful and push the coffee cart to the sink and wash everything. That'll be your job interview."

Jason laughed out loud. "The real Leona finally emerges. All business and bossiness. I'm surprised you can get anyone to stay working for you. You even make the volunteers do a job interview," he teased, glancing at Annie, hoping she would back him up.

Annie was chopping and stirring and pretended to ignore their interaction. She wasn't sure what to make of this Jason guy. He showed up after she found all of her framed photographs strewn around the apartment. Did he do it? Who was he, anyway? *Don't trust anyone* repeated over and over in her head. But she snuck a peak at him working and her body reacted to his maleness even if her brain tried to ignore the rush of feelings.

They all fell into an easy rhythm working on different projects in the café; Leona mixing up another batch of sweetness, Annie finishing the chili and starting the chickpea salad; and Mia manning the ice cream window.

Finally, as Jason pushed the cleaned and organized coffee cart back to its position, he asked Annie, "What's the deal with the knife that was found earlier?"

"You didn't hear about the murder?"

"Yes, I did, and you think the knife is connected?"

"Maybe. I was told Max was stabbed."

"What about Tyler Johnson, the police chief? Who is this other guy taking away possible evidence?"

"He's a detective and he's been investigating the art gallery where Max, the victim, was an owner. He followed Max here to Catfish Cove. He's working with Tyler," Annie explained.

Jason nodded. "What are you mixing up there? Do you need a guinea pig to taste test it?"

"It's Chubby Chickpea Salad. Are you brave enough to try it?" Annie challenged him.

"Definitely. It sounds delicious to a vegetarian."

Annie's eyes popped open wide. "You're a vegetarian?"

"Guilty as charged. Why are you so surprised?" His lips curved into a smile.

"Usually, you big strong macho men are carnivores." Annie's face heated up again. She lost count of how many times Jason got her flustered. For some reason, he managed to keep her off balance and she didn't like it. She needed to have a chat with her body to quit reacting like she was a teenager with a crush.

She put a scoop of the chick pea salad in a bowl and slid it in front of Jason. "Tell me what you think."

"Don't worry, I'm known for my brutal honesty. And the vegetarian thing? That's only one of the many surprises about me." He sampled a big bite, chewing slowly and deliberately as if he was a famous food critic. "Very good. It could use a bit more lemon, or serve a lemon wedge on the side."

"That's actually a good idea. Thanks," she said grudgingly.

"I like the name too. You made that up?"

"I can't take credit for the name. Max's son liked to name my creations when I was living with him."

"Ahh. Another piece of the puzzle revealed."

After Jason devoured the chickpea salad sample and Annie was busy cleaning up some dirty bowls, he whispered something to Leona before leaving the café.

Tyler, JC and Dylan stopped at the ice cream window. "Can we still get a cone?" JC asked Mia.

"Sure. What flavor do you want?"

Dylan asked for mint chocolate chip with hot fudge sauce in a cup with the cone on top. "How about you JC?"

"I'll pass." She laughed. "Dylan will need help finishing this."

Tyler caught Annie's attention and glanced at the door. She nodded and waited for Tyler to walk inside.

"Do you have a few minutes to show me those photos you took of the chili mess?"

"Come on back to Leona's office." Annie got her camera and scrolled to the photos she'd taken the day before and handed her camera to Tyler. "Here they are."

"Wow. That's a big mess! Any idea who would do this?"

Annie shrugged. "I think it's connected to whoever killed Max. Are you making any progress on that?"

"Not really. Every lead ends in a dead end. We haven't even found the murder weapon yet." Tyler put the camera down on Leona's desk.

"What about the knife Detective Jaffrey took a few hours ago?"

Tyler's head jerked around to stare at Annie. "What knife?"

"Mom found a knife with the tip of the blade broken off. It fell off the book shelves when she was straightening them up. Detective Jaffrey put it in an evidence bag and said he was getting it checked to see if it was the murder weapon."

Tyler clenched his jaw. "I hate it when outsiders come in. They think they can ignore the local police and leave us out of the loop. Next time there's something important, please call me, okay?"

"Definitely. I thought you were working together on this."

"I'm going to check into this right now. I wonder if that's why everything I've followed up on has gone nowhere."

Annie took hold of Tyler's arm and whispered, "Listen, Tyler. I know I can trust you and there's a couple other things I want to share with you, but not here. Can you stop by my apartment later? Bring JC too if you want. I don't want her to think I'm up to something behind her back. You know, because of our history and all."

"I don't like the sound of this and I'd prefer not to wait, but maybe you're right. This is too public. We'll swing by your apartment later." Tyler turned to leave but stopped and asked, "I noticed Jason Hunter hanging around the cafe, what's up with that?"

"Beats me. He even volunteered to keep the coffee pots filled tomorrow. What's the deal with him anyway? He's a big question mark for me."

"I heard he used to work for the FBI. To tell you the truth, I don't have a clue what he does. He hardly ever comes around Catfish Cove anymore. Leona could probably fill you in better than I can. She's been friends with him for quite a while. I think his father had something to do with her getting out of jail way back when we were still toddlers."

"That's something I can never get her to talk to me about," Annie said wistfully.

Chapter 16

Leona insisted on dropping Annie at her apartment instead of letting her walk home. With all the craziness of the last couple days she said it seemed safer that way.

"See you tomorrow morning, early, so we can whip up a few more batches of goodies before the customers start flooding in," Annie told Leona as she got out of the mustang. "Thanks for the ride. It's been a long day, and as much as I love to walk, the ride was a treat."

Leona gunned her car after she turned the car around, laughing and waving.

Annie hoped she wouldn't find any drama inside as she unlocked the front door. She didn't think she'd be able to deal with one more problem today. She was stunned when her door opened and she found a vase filled with fresh red and yellow tulips sitting smack in the middle of her table. Her hand covered her chest. Her favorite flowers. Who had done this? A smiling face turned from the counter holding a steaming pizza.

"I'm speechless."

"That's fine. Sit down while I pour you a glass of wine. I'm not much of a cook but I can figure out how to stick a premade pizza in the oven."

Annie sat after she picked up Smokey to cuddle. "How did you know I would be walking in exactly when the pizza was ready to come out of the oven?"

"You caught me. I had a little help from Leona." Jason handed Annie a glass of wine. "You prefer red, right?" He clinked his glass against hers. "Look around on your walls."

Annie tore her eyes from the tulips to see her photographs were all rematted and back in their frames. "You did all this? For me?"

"Good tenants are hard to find and I'd like to keep you here."

"I'm glad you think I'm a good tenant. One disaster after another has followed me ever since I arrived."

"Well, forget about that for the rest of the night and try to relax." He expertly sliced the pizza, sliding a piece onto a plate for Annie.

"Vegetarian I see. My favorite—peppers, onions and mushrooms. I'm touched by your generosity, Mr. Hunter."

Jason sat down across from Annie and held up his glass. "Cheers."

A comfortable silence filled the room as they ate the pizza and sipped their wine.

Annie finished her wine and set her glass down. "I've been wondering, Mr. Hunter, what is it that you do?"

"Besides making dinner for my tenant?" he answered with his lips turned up in a teasing smile.

"Besides the pizza, flowers and repairing my photographs. Yes. You're not getting off the hook that easily."

His gaze moved to the view out the window. Lights twinkled in the homes around the lake. "I find things."

Annie laughed, nearly choking on the bite of pizza she just put in her mouth. "You find things? What kind of things?"

"Anything really. Whatever someone needs help finding."

Annie rested her chin on her hand and scrunched up her mouth. "Are you any good?"

With eyebrows raised, Jason brought his eyes back to stare into Annie's. "Yes. I always find what I'm looking for, but that doesn't guarantee my customer is happy in the end."

"Why not?"

"Uncovering one thing quite often leads to discovering more secrets that people aren't always ready for." Jason shifted in his seat. "Why the interest? Is there something you need to find?"

"Yes, but I'm not positive I want to find it."

Jason nodded. "It's good to know what you want before you start the search."

"The search is started and I won't stop. It's just, well, you wouldn't understand."

"Try me." He focused his complete attention on Annie's face. "I'm guessing you're searching for a truth about yourself."

Annie's jaw dropped. She stood up, carrying her plate to the counter, saying nothing, but wondering how he could figure that out about her so quickly.

"Those searches are the most difficult. But also can be the most rewarding."

A knock on the door sliced through the tension in the room.

Jason stood up. "Are you expecting someone? I need to leave now anyway." He bowed to Annie. "I'm happy to have been of service to you tonight."

"Thanks for all of this," she said, waving her hand around the room. "I'm expecting a friend." Annie smiled and felt a tingle when Jason smiled back and gently traced his fingers down her arm as he walked to the door.

Tyler and JC passed Jason as he left and they entered Annie's apartment. JC's eyebrow was cocked in an expression of curiosity as she took in the wine bottle, pizza, and flowers on the table. "Are we interrupting something?"

Annie flapped her hand dismissively. "No, not at all. I can't figure that guy out. He shows up at odd moments, like he's always keeping an eye on me. Where's Dylan?"

JC made herself comfortable on the couch, scooping Smokey up into her arms. "Dylan's at a friend's birthday party. We need to pick him up in about a half hour. Cute kitty. Where'd he come from?"

"I found him at the café, locked in one of the cupboards. That's where the new name, Black Cat Café, came from. Tyler, sit down. Want a beer or something?"

They both shook their heads. "No thanks. You wanted to tell me something, Annie?" Tyler asked, sitting, but not relaxing back into the soft cushions.

She sat down across from them, handing the note she had taken from Max's pocket to Tyler. "I saw this after I found Max dead."

Tyler read the note. "Who do you think he was talking about?"

"That's the problem. I don't have a clue. He says not to trust anyone, but I shared this with my mom, Leona, Martha, and now you two."

"Where did you find this note?"

Annie looked down at the floor and sighed deeply. "I took it out of his pocket. Once I read it, I was too worried to show anyone right away. But there's been too many other weird things happening."

Tyler leaned forward. "What else? Tell me everything."

"The chili being dumped out, like someone was trying to sabotage our opening day for some reason. And this afternoon, when I came home for a break, all my photographs were torn apart like someone was searching for something hidden between the photos and the backing."

"Looking for what?"

"I'm not sure." Annie wouldn't meet Tyler's questioning eyes.

"Annie, what else haven't you told me?" He moved across the room, took her hand and forced her to look at him. "You're hiding something else, I know you too well."

She nodded. "This morning, I hung one of my photographs at the café and it wouldn't hang right." She looked from Tyler to JC. "When I adjusted the wire, I noticed a bulge behind the paper backing and found a bag of drugs hidden there. Later is when I found all my other photographs torn apart."

"Where are the drugs now?"

"Hidden. No one will find them. I want to figure out why Max or someone else hid it behind my photograph. I don't think he was involved in anything illegal. I think he followed me here trying to make it right. Whatever that was."

"Have you told Detective Neil Jaffrey all this?" Tyler asked with an edge in his voice.

"No. I haven't told him anything about this stuff."

Tyler dropped Annie's hand. "Good. Keep it that way. The less people who know, the better. I'm still waiting to get the information about the knife that you told me about. The awl wasn't the murder weapon but there was blood on the point and Max's fingerprints on the handle which is suspicious."

Annie nodded, not telling Tyler that Detective Jaffrey already shared that information with her. She could sense that Tyler was annoyed with the detective and there was no reason to add more fuel to that fire.

JC stood up. "We need to pick Dylan up. Are you going to be alright tonight, Annie?"

Smokey wrapped his thin body around Annie's legs, purring loudly. She bent down and picked him up. "I'll be fine. Smokey's good company."

Annie stretched out on her couch with Smokey curled on her chest, purring contentedly. She let her mind wander back to Max, trying to think of any indication of his involvement with the drugs hidden behind her photographs.

"Smokey, what do you think? Max took my photos to the gallery to frame them for the show. Why did he put them in my car? Maybe someone else tampered with them after he was done and he saw them and decided to hide them in my car. When I disappeared, he had to find me and get it back. Vincent followed Max here and Detective Jaffrey followed Vincent? How is Jake connected? Anyone else?" She started to doze off when a voice startled her.

Chapter 17

Annie bolted upright, sending Smokey sliding on the wood floor as his claws dug in for traction on his way to hide under the couch. "What are you doing here?"

"I asked you a question, Annie. Where's the other bag of pot?" Roy sat in a chair facing Annie, looking haggard and exhausted.

"What are you talking about?" Annie's mind raced, wondering why her father was here, for one thing, and how did he know about the pot?

"I found everything behind these photos but there's one more. Where did you hide it?"

Annie shut her mouth, which had hung open after the realization of what her father told her sunk in. He was the one who broke into her apartment. "You tore my photos apart?"

"You are so naïve. Where's the last one?" Roy sat with his elbows on his knees and his head hanging down. "There's nothing behind your photograph at the café."

Annie was wide awake now. "How are you involved in this?"

"You don't want to know. Just help me out here so this nightmare can end."

"You killed Max?"

"He was stupid to put you in danger. I'm trying to mop up his mess."

Annie stood up, her hands clenched so tightly, her nails dug into her hands. "Get out. I hate you," she said in a controlled but deadly tone. Max's words screamed in her brain—don't trust anyone.

Roy slowly straightened. "Have it your way, but it won't end well."

He walked out, slamming the door behind him.

She rushed to the door, locking it and sliding a chair under the door knob for extra security. The windows she had loved earlier turned into enemies now, allowing anyone to see in. Turning off the lights, she carried Smokey into the bedroom, closed the curtains and fell into a restless sleep.

***

Waking in a pitch black room, Annie's first thought was what an awful nightmare she'd had. Unfortunately, as sleep left her brain, the reality of her father's involvement in Max's murder sank in. Was he the murderer or was he helping someone else? Time would answer that question, she thought.

Annie opened her curtains to the sun just rising over the water. Time to get to the café and help Leona get ready for the day. Today was the fishing derby and, from what she could remember from when she was younger, the Saturday of the Spring Celebration was the busiest day. Tourists would be swarming through town and The Black Cat Café would be swamped for sure.

She checked that Smokey had fresh food and water before grabbing her keys and heading to her car. No walking to town after the visit from her father and the unknown dangers facing her.

A shadow crossed in front of Jason's kitchen window, the window facing Annie's apartment. She shivered and picked up her pace, hoping her car would cooperate this morning. It turned over on the first try and Annie let out the breath she had been holding in. "One thing going right today," she said to herself.

What took her about twenty minutes to walk was only a five minute coast down the hill into the parking lot of the Cove's Corner building. She pulled in next to Leona's mustang, slung her camera over her shoulder and jogged inside.

The comforting aroma of coffee and baking cinnamon rolls made her smile as soon as she opened the door. Food makes everything feel safer, she thought.

The Fabric Stash and Clay Design were dark and quiet but a welcoming light and rock 'n roll music came out of The Black Cat Café. "Leona!" Annie shouted over the music. "When do you sleep?"

Leona danced her way to the radio, turning it down, before answering. "Sleep? Who needs sleep when the best coffee in town is right here? We can sleep when we're dead."

"Listen. My father showed up at my house last night looking for the last bag of pot. Hopefully, we get a chance to sleep before we're dead like Max."

Leona put her arm around Annie. "Slow down, Red. What else did he say?"

"Not much. He tore apart my framed photos in my apartment yesterday and found more drugs there. He said I'm naïve and things will turn out badly if I don't give him the last one."

"Did you tell him you found it?"

"No." They both looked at the photograph hanging on the café wall and saw that it hung at an angle. Annie got to it first, flipping it over to see the backing gone. "At least he didn't pull the whole thing apart. Maybe that last bag will be our bargaining chip."

Leona whispered to Annie, "Don't turn around now, but here comes trouble. We have to figure out how to buy some time."

"Leona. Are you in on this too?" Roy shouted.

"Whatever are you talking about?" Leona answered in a sickening sweet voice.

"Don't play cute with me." He glanced at the books. "I'll search through every book if I have to. Make a mess of this whole place."

Leona laughed. "No need for that, it would hurt you too. You own the building and my success is your success. Let's get through today and we'll talk."

Roy frowned. "Eight tonight. Here. Don't be late." He turned and left.

Leona leaned on the counter. "He's one stressed out guy. Do you think he killed Max?"

"The thought crossed my mind."

The oven timer shrieked making Leona and Annie jump. "Back to work, Red. The floodgates will open in an hour."

Leona took out her cinnamon rolls and slid in another batch of blueberry muffins. Annie loaded the pastry case and organized the breakfast cart and coffee/tea cart. She made a note to mix up another batch of granola when she had time. A soothing rhythm helped to calm her jittery nerves.

Annie looked up when the door opened. Danny stood just inside, holding his baseball cap and wringing it with both hands. "Am I too early to get some coffee?"

Leona waved him over. "Come on in. We aren't officially open yet but there's always coffee for you. Help yourself. Do you want something to eat too?"

Danny grinned. "You're too good to me, Leona. I'd love one of your blueberry muffins with the streusel topping. I would be a contented man if I could eat them every day. Nothing beats the sweet and sour burst in every bite." He poured coffee and slid onto one of the counter stools. "What do your customers think of the books?"

"They're a big hit," Annie answered happily. "Your shelves add a comfy atmosphere to the café."

He sipped his coffee. "The fishing derby starts at seven. First prize is a new rod and reel and I sure would like to win this year and replace my old pole."

"I heard they stocked the lake with some mighty big trout. If I wasn't working here, I'd be out there competing too," Leona said. "And you know what I'd do if I won?"

Danny shook his head and took a big bite of the muffin.

"I'd give that rod and reel to you, Danny Davis. I can't think of anyone more deserving than you."

Danny blushed and smiled from ear to ear. "Aww, Leona. Thanks. You always make me feel like a million bucks. You have any more work for me?"

"I wish I did, but no, not at the moment."

Annie said, "I have a job for you. I need a table and a couple of chairs for my deck. Oh yeah, and a bird feeder for my cat to watch from the window. I like to think of it as cat T.V."

"Sure thing, Annie. I could start on Monday." He set his empty coffee cup on the counter and pressed his finger into the muffin crumbs, getting every last bit. "Thanks for letting me sneak in early, that's just the boost I need before I start fishing."

"Good luck. We'll be rooting for you."

Danny headed to the door and stopped. "I remembered something about the night when I fell asleep in your office."

Leona and Annie stopped what they were doing and waited for Danny to continue.

"One of the voices I heard arguing was your father, Annie."

"Are you sure?"

"I heard him yelling at you before I came in this morning and I'm positive it was one of the voices I heard that night."

"At Jake's Clay Design shop?" Leona asked.

"Yeah. And they sounded really angry, just like Roy sounded when he was in here."

Chapter 18

Karen, from the animal shelter, walked in at seven on the dot with Mia. "Sorry I didn't stop by yesterday but there was a constant stream of people looking to adopt and I couldn't get away," Karen told Leona. "How did your opening day turn out?"

"Busy. We sold out of a lot of baked goods and spent the afternoon restocking. Help yourself to some coffee, and there's granola on the breakfast cart if you're hungry, or a muffin," Leona explained.

"I'm getting something to go, so I'll grab a coffee and a blueberry muffin. I'm off to get my space set up for the animals that are ready for adoption. This is usually a great weekend to find homes for my boys and girls."

"Don't put Baxter in that line up," Leona said with panic written all over her face. "He's moving in with me as soon as I can take him."

Karen laughed. "Don't worry about your precious Baxter. He's got a few more days to wait before he can go home with you. Annie, any chance of stopping by to take some photos of the newly adopted dogs and cats and their new families?"

"I'd love to." Annie looked at Leona. "I guess it depends on how busy it is here. I'll swing by when there's a slow stretch. Are you around all day?"

"All day," Karen confirmed.

The families of the fishermen and women in the derby streamed into the café looking for coffee and something yummy. The parents already looked stressed and in need of a caffeine fix and the kids were hyper from the excitement of the activities, and also from an overload of sugar, Annie thought. It didn't stop them from begging for blueberry muffins and other sweets. Annie loaded up the pastry case and wondered if Jason was going to follow through with his offer to man the coffee cart. They certainly could use the extra hands.

Mia chatted with each customer as they stopped at the cash register to pay and she kept the line moving steadily. Most headed out the door to the deck so they could watch the activity on the lake. A few people stopped at the freebrary, browsing the titles, finding a treasure, and returning with something from their car to replace what they took. The book swap was catching on and seemed to be popular.

Annie had her hands full of fruit and yogurt, making smoothies for several customers, when she glanced up and saw Jason casually walk into the café. He nodded to Annie, poured himself a coffee and made himself comfortable on a stool at the counter.

"I'm all yours, tell me what to do," he said, then kept his eyes on her over the rim of his coffee mug.

The annoying rush of heat in her checks irritated Annie, even if the sound of having him all to herself appealed to the rest of her body. "Keep an eye on the coffee and hot water for tea. There should always be one pot with fresh coffee and one brewing. Refill the water for tea as needed. That should keep you out of trouble."

Jason's lip twitched slightly as he tried not to laugh at Annie's blushing face. He saluted her and left the stool to check the coffee pots.

Annie couldn't help but keep an eye on Jason as she served muffins and scones to the customers. He finds things, she thought. Was he searching for something now or was he in between jobs? Maybe he would be able to help her find her birth parents. She wasn't ready to open up about that to him though. Not yet.

Vincent and Jake came into the café arguing about Jake's pottery shipment. Annie listened carefully, hoping to hear something that might help solve Max's murder or uncover a clue about how the drugs ended up hidden behind her photographs.

Vincent tried to keep his voice down, but Annie caught enough of the conversation. "I don't care about the last one, these boxes need to be shipped out today."

The last one? What last one was he talking about? The last bag of drugs that Annie had? As they stood in front of the pastry case, Annie glanced at Jake's belt and saw his knife holster was empty. It could be in his shop, she thought. Or did he lose it in the café?

"Annie. Are you paying attention?"

She realized Jake's mouth was moving as he talked to her but she hadn't heard a word he said. "Sorry. What did you want?"

"That blueberry muffin." He pointed to the left side of the tray. "The big one with all the streusel on top and blueberries bursting out the side. To go."

Annie handed it to Jake in a paper bag. "Anything for you, Vincent?" She tried her hardest to be polite even though she couldn't stand the guy.

He sneered at Annie. "You know what I want, and it's not in your pastry case."

Jason was adding more water to heat for tea but Annie could tell that he was following every word that Vincent said. His demeanor changed from friendly and relaxed to stern and focused. She shivered and knew she didn't want to be on his bad side.

The crowd started to thin out a bit after the initial surge when they opened the café door at seven. Annie busied herself preparing all the meats and veggies for the lunch rush so she'd be able to whip the sandwiches together as quickly as possible. If the morning rush was any indication, she expected the lunch crowd to be much busier than yesterday.

Detective Jaffrey showed up, helping himself to coffee and granola. He made himself comfy at one of the booths just vacated by a family of four. Leona found time to slide into the booth and do a bit of flirting. They leaned their heads together as if they were sharing their deepest secrets until she laughed and made her way back behind the counter.

Leona gave the chili a good stir and turned the burners off. "Can you help me pour this into the warmers on the soup cart?"

As Leona tipped the pot, Annie carefully ladled the steaming hot chili into the warmers to avoid any splashing. She whispered to Leona, "We need to search Clay Design and find out what Jake is packing into those boxes."

"Do you think it's drugs?" Leona said with a gleam in her eyes.

"Maybe. I heard him talking to Vincent, and something isn't right with those two. Plus, Jake's knife wasn't in his holster."

"Okay. Reconnaissance mission. I'm in. We'll need a distraction to flush them out of the shop. Martha and Mia can help with that if necessary. Let's plan it for after lunch. Oh, I almost forgot, Detective Jaffrey needs to talk to you. Says he received some information you'll be interested in." Leona scrunched one eyebrow. "Two hot guys in here and they both have their eye on you. You need to decide which one you'll let me go after."

Annie laughed. "You're full of baloney, Leona. You do whatever you want, you always do. But don't you think they're both a bit young for you?"

"Nope. Not at all." She winked and nodded toward the detective. "That's the one I want."

"Well, go for him then, and good luck."

"What are you two laughing about over here?" Mia asked as she helped herself to a small bowl of chili.

"Your sister has her eye on Detective Jaffrey. Poor guy," Annie teased. "I'll put in a good word for you."

Annie slid into the booth opposite the detective. "You have some information for me?"

"I think so. My office found some mail that came for Max."

Annie felt her heart skip a beat. "Why are you telling me this?"

"Was he helping you with a search?"

Annie stared at the detective silently.

"Your name is in the document."

"Can I see it?" She barely managed to get the words out.

"How about I swing by your apartment later? I don't have it with me now."

Annie nodded. "I'll call and let you know when I'm home."

"Sure." Detective Jaffrey covered Annie's hand with his warm fingers. "You're as white as a ghost. What do you think it is?"

"I'm afraid to find out."

Chapter 19

Annie was frozen in the booth wondering if she would finally find out who her birth parents were. Weeks ago, Max told her he was getting closer, then the lead dried up. This might be the information he had been waiting for. A tear ran down her cheek and plopped on the table.

"I didn't mean to upset you."

Her eyes focused on the detective's face. "It's not your fault." She slid out of the booth. "I'll call and let you know when I'm home." she repeated.

Annie told Leona she needed some fresh air. She grabbed her camera and headed toward the door but Mia stopped her. "Are you alright?"

"Yeah, Mom. I'm going to visit Karen and the shelter dogs for a few minutes. I promised I'd take photos with their new families." But really, Annie needed some time to herself.

Annie used her camera as a barrier between her feelings and the world. It had worked before and it would work again. Once she focused through the lens, her attention was on the image framed inside instead of the feelings she wanted to avoid.

The fishermen were about done with the derby and she snapped photos of the interesting characters with their gear and catches. Boats bobbed along the docks and little kids ran up and down, excited to see what their mom or dad caught.

Annie's camera found Danny's smiling face as he held up a big trout. She snapped quickly before he saw her and hid the true happiness on his face from the camera. When he stepped up to the scale, the crowd held their breath and erupted as one when the indicator stopped on nineteen and a half pounds. Danny's fish tipped the scales as the biggest of the day, a real beauty. Annie snapped away, lost in the excitement and Danny's happiness.

A light touch on her shoulder and Jason's voice brought her out of her zone. "I don't think he could be any happier, could he?"

Annie smiled to herself. What was it about this guy that made her nerves tingle, she wondered. "I think everyone is sharing his happiness." She passed Jason her camera to show him the photos she captured.

"You have an incredible eye and perfect timing capturing the moment. Beautiful work." He gave her camera back. "You left in a hurry. Is there a problem?"

"No." She turned away, not wanting him to guess that she was lying. "I promised Karen, from the animal shelter, that I would take some photos of her dogs and cats with their new adoptive families. Come on." Annie reached for Jason's arm, pulling him along with her. "Maybe you'll get sucked into volunteering at the shelter too after you meet everyone."

"I'm not sure I like the sound of this," he protested. "I haven't met a homeless dog yet that I didn't fall in love with."

"Great!"

Karen had a portable fence around a grassy area with volunteers standing with each dog ready for adoption. Cats were in kennels, mewing, hoping for attention from the many people walking around.

Annie started to click photos, forgetting that she had pulled Jason along with her. As her eye behind the lens moved around the enclosure, she stopped when Jason came into view, crouching down beside Roxy, the dog Annie had walked when she went to the shelter with Leona. Jason seemed to be having a heart to heart talk with the sweet dog and the tip of Roxy's tail wagged tentatively.

Annie knew she got several amazing shots before she walked over to Jason and Roxy. "She's a perfect sweetheart and I heard she's great with cats."

"Annie Fisher, you found my weakness. The only problem is that I travel too much to adopt a dog. It wouldn't be fair to the dog," he said as he stroked Roxy's silky head.

"Well, you do have a tenant that also has a weakness for this four legged beauty," Annie hinted.

"Give me your camera and I'll see if the two of you make an adorable couple." Jason took Annie's camera before she had a chance to protest. He backed away and Roxy put her two front paws on Annie's side and looked into her face with big soft milk chocolate eyes. Annie crouched down so Roxy's face was even with hers as Jason clicked away with her camera.

Annie stood up laughing. "Okay. Enough! I don't want to break my favorite lens."

Jason was already looking at what he took. "Nothing here to break your lens, only someone's heart."

Annie felt a rush of heat to her face as she stumbled over her words. "What are you talking about?"

"Roxy's heart. Take a look. That dog has 'I love you' oozing out of every hair on her face. You two are meant for each other." He handed the camera back to Annie so she could see the photos for herself.

She felt her face get even hotter as she realized she was hoping Jason meant she would break his heart. What was she thinking? He probably had a girlfriend in every town he visited. Someone as handsome as

Jason would have every female draping themselves over him.

Karen came over to see what Jason and Annie were discussing. "I hope you convinced her that she needs Roxy in her life."

"I'm working on her." Jason elbowed Annie. "Just say yes. I can see it in your face that you want her to move in."

With a big smile on her face, Annie nodded. "Yes! Now, give me my camera back. I want to get some more shots before I head back to the café."

"Take as long as you need. I'll go back and help Leona and tell her the good news."

Annie took photos of the people and their newly adopted pets. Everyone had huge smiles on their faces, including Karen who looked happiest of all. "This is one of the best days we've ever had. Ten dogs found homes, including Roxy, and a dozen cats. That opens up spaces for more dogs and cats waiting for room to get into my shelter."

"You have a waiting list?"

Karen laughed. "I'm a no kill shelter so, yes, there are always animals waiting for a spot."

"I'll put these photos on a disk for you and you can use them on your website or whatever you want."

Karen hugged Annie. "You have no idea how much this will help. Once people see the true spirit of these animals shining through they always find a home. And you made a good decision with Roxy. She's a special one. I'll keep her until you get done with work. Stop by the shelter later."

Annie started walking back to the café when she noticed Vincent carrying boxes out of the Cove's Corner building and heading to his car. She hurried inside. "Leona, we have to get into Jake's Clay Design shop before all the boxes are gone."

"Perfect timing, I just put a batch of muffins in the oven. Ask your mom if she's okay here by herself for a few minutes, and get Martha too if she can leave her shop."

Annie explained to Mia what she wanted to do and Mia was all on board. "If I see Vincent walking in, I'll call him into the café to give you some more time."

Martha was busy with customers so Annie went into Clay Design alone, assuming Leona wouldn't be too far behind. "Jake, where's your new best friend Vincent?" Annie asked and saw Jake flinch at the mention of Vincent's name.

"What's it to you?" He continued to tape up boxes, doing his best to ignore Annie. "Don't you have someplace else you need to be? Like, anyplace but here? I'm busy and not in the mood for chatting."

Leona sauntered in. "That's too bad, Jake, because we have a few questions for you." She walked over and pulled out a piece of pottery from a box that wasn't taped yet.

"Hey, what do you think you're doing?" Vincent reached to grab the pot from Leona.

That gave Annie the opening to rip open the box he was working on and search inside. She pulled out a coffee mug stuffed with a bag of drugs. "I knew it." She held the bag up for Leona to see.

Leona grabbed Jake by the collar of his shirt. She leaned in, mere inches from his nose. "Tell us what's going on. Did you kill Max? We found a knife that looks a lot like yours in the café."

Jake's face went completely white. "I didn't kill him. Vincent is blackmailing me. I knew my knife was missing. He must have stolen it to make me look guilty," he pleaded with Leona. "You've got to believe me."

She twisted his shirt tighter. "Why should we believe you?"

"I know about the drugs hidden behind Annie's photographs. If we work together, we can nail Vincent and get him locked up once and for all."

Leona practically picked Jake up off the floor before letting go of his shirt. "Okay. Give us something."

"All the drugs are packed in these boxes of my pottery. Everything will be in his car. Make sure you get to him before he leaves town."

"And what about Max?" Annie asked

"Max wanted out. I don't even know if he was part of the drug connection or just wanted out of the partnership with Vincent. I want out. Everyone wants out but Vincent has something on us so we can't walk away. Max tried to and look what happened. But, I swear, I didn't kill him." His eyes went from Leona to Annie and back again.

"How did you even get involved? It's not like Catfish Cove is next door to Vincent's gallery," Annie pointed out.

Jake shook his head. "I was looking for a gallery to show my work and I contacted the wrong one. It's complicated."

They heard Mia's voice in the hallway. "Vincent? Can you help me for a minute?"

"I'm busy." His footsteps continued toward Clay Design without slowing down.

Leona, Annie and Jake held their breath as Vincent stormed into the shop. "What's going on in here?"

Chapter 20

Vincent glared at Annie. She turned around, happy that her mother had called out his name, giving her enough warning to be prepared for Vincent coming into Clay Design. She had a split second to stuff the bag of drugs back into the mug before riveting her eyes on him.

"You look terrible, Vincent. You should think about crawling back under the rock you came from and try to get over whatever is ailing you." Turning her attention back to Jake, she asked, "How long will it take to get the new mugs done for the café? Leona and I think the pot you gave us with the black cat design would be a hot seller on coffee mugs with all the tourists."

"I, ah, could make about dozen for next week. How does that sound?"

"Perfect," Annie said. "Come on Leona. We'd better get back to the café. Business is booming."

Vincent moved in front of Annie to block her path. "You think you're clever, don't you? Watch out."

Leona pushed between them like an overprotective mama bear. "Are you threatening us, you little snake? You don't know who you're messing with. I could break you in two like a dried twig. Why are you even here in town?" Her eyes traveled over Vincent from head to toe. "Be careful or your shiny suit might need a trip to the cleaners."

Leona knocked him aside with her elbow as she walked out of Clay Design with Annie leaning against her.

"Did you see his face? Calling him a snake is an insult to all the snakes in Catfish Cove." Annie bent over double laughing so hard she had to cross her legs so she didn't wet her pants. "You made him mad, Leona."

"Good. We've got that meeting tonight at eight with Roy. I think Jake and Vincent need an invitation too. Get the three of them fighting with each other."

"What about Tyler and Detective Jaffrey?"

"Not yet. Let's keep them out of this for now." Leona stopped. "Hey, what's this I heard about you adopting Roxy?"

"Someone has a big mouth." Annie smiled. "You should have seen Jason with the dogs. I think he wanted to adopt her but he said he travels too much. What's his story? He finds things?"

Leona shrugged. "Jason and I got pretty close when his dad helped get my sentence reduced when I went to jail at eighteen. I don't know what strings he pulled but he made me swear I would straighten my act out or else. Jason was just a kid then and we've always stayed in touch. I think it's more like he makes sure I keep my promise to his dad."

"So nothing ever romantic between the two of you?"

Leona grinned. "Nope. He's more like an annoying little brother that always shows up to spoil the fun." Her face broke into a wicked grin. "Are you interested? I can tell he's a bit, shall I say, taken with you?"

A scream and loud crash made both Leona and Annie sprint into the café. Mia held her arm and muffins were scattered on the floor around her feet.

"What happened?" Leona and Annie both asked at the same time.

"I was rushing, taking two pans out at once and one hot tray flopped onto my arm. Stupid."

Jason wrapped a wet cloth around the red burn on the inside of Mia's arm. "I'll take her to the emergency room, you two can stay here and finish up the baking."

"Are you sure?" Annie asked, full of worry.

Mia waved off the concern. "I'll be fine. You two need to get ready for tomorrow."

"This day is flying by. I'm going to close up the café which will piss Roy off, but since we're short-handed now, that can't be helped. Business is tapering off anyway." Leona picked up the muffin tray, which had thankfully landed right side up. "This isn't a total loss. Only a few popped out, the rest can be sold."

Annie began to dump ingredients into a large mixing bowl for a batch of granola. "Once this is in the oven, I'll mix up another recipe of Chubby Chickpea Salad. It was a huge hit today."

"I'll finish this batch of cinnamon rolls, but they can sit in the fridge until tomorrow morning. I'll stick them in the oven when I get here. The cinnamon smell is about the best aroma to greet everyone's noses first thing. After you finish the salad and granola, aren't you going over to the animal shelter to pick up your new family member? I'm sure she'd rather be with you than stuck in the kennel."

Annie did a little dance of happiness. "I can't believe I've only been back in Catfish Cove for less than a week and I have a job, an awesome apartment and a dog and cat. I wasn't sure I'd be staying, but these events kind of made up my mind for me."

"Don't forget finding a body and the drugs," Leona added.

"Well, yeah, there's that too, but I would rather focus on the good parts of being back here. I want to check on Mom before I pick up Roxy. How about Baxter? Are you going to visit him?"

"That's my plan. Let's get this done so we can head out for some fun."

The radio blasted Leona's favorite oldies songs as they worked efficiently. Martha knocked on the door, holding up a package. "Hey, hon, let me in."

Annie wiped her hands on a towel and unlocked the door for Martha.

"I'm popping in to show you some more aprons I made for the two of you. What do you think?"

Annie held it up in front of herself. "You're so creative. I love this big black cat sitting on the front of the apron. And the bright yellow background really makes it pop. It's a lot like the sign Danny made."

"I couldn't find enough of the other fabric so I cut out this cat design and appliquéd it on the background."

"If you can make this design smaller and put it on tea towels, I'll sell them here along with the mugs Jake is making for us," Leona said.

"Great idea. I can whip some up in no time at all. How about some placemats too?"

"Of course." Leona looked around her café. "I'll call Danny and ask him to build me a table next to the cash register to display your creations. Keep some for your store, too."

Martha waved her hand. "I don't get a fraction of the traffic through my shop that you get coming through the café. I'm happy for you to be my outlet. Besides, if I get too many customers, it cuts into my sewing time."

"Listen," Annie said, changing the subject. "My father is coming here tonight at eight to get that bag I found behind my photograph."

"Roy? How's he involved?"

"I wish I knew the answer to that question. We're still trying to figure it out. Jake is involved too, but he said Vincent is blackmailing him and he wants to help us. I wonder if Vincent found something on my father too, but I can't imagine what. Max must have had information he was trying to get to me before he was murdered. Danny heard arguing the night before Max was killed and he told us he recognized Roy's voice. I bet it was Jake, Vincent and Roy arguing the night before Max was murdered."

Martha clapped her hands together. "I bet the creepy Vincent character is the murderer. Jake can be abrasive and Roy is a jerk, but can you see them murdering anyone?"

Leona finished up the cinnamon rolls and put them in the fridge. "You never know what someone will do when they are desperate. We need to be extra careful tonight. Roy wants those drugs and maybe that will be the end of it, but if Vincent is blackmailing everyone, who knows what he'll do to cover his tracks. Maybe we should tell Detective Jaffrey or Tyler about our meeting."

"No, let's keep to our original plan." Annie said. "What could happen with so many people together? Vincent won't be able to kill all of us."

Martha folded the aprons and put them on the counter. "How about if I hide in my shop with the lights off and keep my cell phone ready to call the police? Just in case."

Annie smiled. "Good idea. But don't park your car here or that will tip Vincent off that you're around." She wondered what her meeting with Detective Jaffrey would reveal. She could always tell him about this other meeting if she decided it was time to trust him.

Chapter 21

Annie and Leona finished cleaning up the café and made a plan to be back early again to get everything ready for Sunday morning. With all the business and preparations for Friday and Saturday, business on Sunday could go either way. All in all, the café was already popular with the locals and tourists. Having so much set up as self-serve took a lot of pressure off Annie and Leona. Mia's help was the touch they needed, but they didn't know if they could count on her help in the morning after she burned her arm.

It was a short drive to the small community hospital. Jason was helping Mia walk out as Annie pulled into the emergency parking area. She hopped out of her car and waved. Mia held up her bandaged arm and waited for Annie to walk to them.

"So, how's the patient?"

"Feeling like a complete idiot. It's a second degree burn with a nasty blister and the doctor gave me strict orders to keep the blister clean and dry, but it should be better in two to three weeks."

"Do you want a ride home?" Annie winked at Jason. "Your chauffer probably has something better to do."

"Sure." Mia thanked Jason and followed Annie to her car.

"I'm glad your arm wasn't burned more severely, Mom."

"I was rushing around and wondering what you and Leona were up to so my focus wasn't on the hot trays. The accident was complete carelessness on my part."

"What's the deal with Jason? Leona told me he's like a brother to her, but I don't ever remember seeing him around."

Leona gazed out the window. "That was around the time you came into my life and Leona and I, well, we didn't hang around a lot back then. I heard Jason's name mentioned, but he wasn't part of my life. I think he's six or seven years older than you."

Annie pulled into the animal shelter. "Good. Karen's car is still here."

Mia gave Annie a puzzled look. "Why are you stopping here?"

"I adopted a dog today. When I went over to take pictures, well, I got more than some great shots."

"Let me see. I love your photos."

Annie handed the camera to her mother. "Is this the dog?" Mia tilted the camera so Annie could see a shot of herself with Roxy.

"Yeah, that's Roxy. Isn't she adorable? I met her the other day when Leona brought me here to meet the dog she wants to adopt."

"Who took this shot?"

"Jason followed me over and he's the one who twisted my arm and got me to say yes. He said he would love to adopt her but he travels too much. Come on, let's get inside before we waste any more time."

Karen was sweeping the front area but leaned the broom on her desk when Mia and Annie walked in. "I was afraid you changed your mind, Annie. Roxy is out back, curled up on her pillow acting depressed. You would have broken her heart if you didn't show up to bring her home."

"You're the second person today to tell me I could break that dog's heart."

Karen's eyebrow went up in question. "Who else made that observation? Was it that handsome man you were with?"

Annie felt her cheeks flush with embarrassment, making Karen and Mia laugh at her. "Yes, as a matter of fact, it was that handsome man." She raised her eyebrows at the two women. "I can't figure him out. He's way too considerate and handsome," she added, "to still be single."

"People don't always find their soul mate right away, honey," Mia explained.

Annie shrugged. "I'm not looking for another relationship anyway. I screwed up my engagement with Tyler, and Max got murdered. No one will want anything to do with me with that history. Everyone will be heading for the hills once they find out about my track record."

"I know someone who can't wait to move in with you," Karen said nodding toward the back room with all the kennels.

That comment brought a huge smile to Annie's face as she headed through the door. "I'll be right back."

And she was. With a happy dog following, watching Annie's every move. "Thanks Karen. I'll be back for a photo shoot soon. Come on Mom. I'll drop you off at home, then get this girl some food and see how she gets along with Smokey."

Roxy jumped into the back seat of Annie's Saab, curling up like it was her usual spot.

"You and dogs," Mia said, smiling as she shook her head. "I'm glad you're back. I don't know anything about Jason but I think you found a soul mate with this girl."

Annie reached over and squeezed her mother's hand. "I'm glad I'm back too. It doesn't matter so much to me anymore if I find my birth parents. You're my mom. The rest won't change anything. Right?"

Mia nodded as a tear slid down her cheek. "Thanks, Annie. You don't know how much that means to me."

"Enough of this emotional stuff. We need to figure out what Roy has up his sleeve."

"What are you talking about?" Mia asked.

"I thought I already told you. He knows about the drugs hidden behind my photographs and we're meeting him tonight at eight at the café. He found all but one of the bags of drugs and thinks I'm going to give him the missing one tonight."

"Are you?"

"No. I think Vincent is behind it all and Jake said he'd help us. Vincent is blackmailing Jake and trying to make him look like he's the murderer."

"Maybe he is. How can you be sure you can trust what Jake tells you?"

"Well, I can't, but if Jake, Vincent and Roy show up, Leona is hoping that one of them will rat on whoever the murderer is. We think Vincent may be blackmailing Roy too. At least, part of me hopes it is that and not something worse."

Mia pursed her lips. "I don't like this. Your plan sounds too iffy and dangerous. What's the backup plan?"

"Martha is going to hide in her shop ready to call the police at the first sign of trouble."

"Okay, I'll be with Martha." Mia got out of Annie's car. "Be careful. I think there is more to this than you can imagine."

Annie looked in the rear view mirror at Roxy who was now sitting like a statue in the middle of the back seat. "What do you think?"

Roxy perked her ears up.

"Okay, we'll head home and see what you think about Smokey."

Fatigue settled in Annie's body. The last few days had been nonstop drama and she couldn't wait for all that to be behind her. She wished she had confidence to leave it all up to Tyler to solve, but she was smack dab in the middle and there was no way she would let herself end up like Max if she didn't work on finding his killer as quickly as possible. She desperately wanted to know how her father got mixed up in all of this with Vincent and Jake. What was the common denominator with all of them, she wondered.

As she pulled into her apartment she was happy that she had about an hour before she needed to go back to the café. She had enough time to get Roxy settled in with Smokey and stretch out on her couch and take a short nap before she called Detective Jaffrey. "Come on girl. On to a new adventure for you."

Her photographs on the walls, the view of the lake, and Smokey and Roxy for company would make this apartment into a home, Annie thought as she walked inside. Smokey took one look at the four-legged intruder with Annie and hid under the couch. Roxy followed the kitten and poked her nose down to investigate, only to be met by a black paw smacking her. Roxy backed up, wagging her tail and sat down to wait for Smokey to make the next move.

Annie couldn't help but smile at the kitten's antics, until her smile was replaced with a gasp as the bathroom door opened with a squeak. Her body tensed. "Who's here?"

Chapter 22

Detective Jaffrey walked out of the bathroom. "Sorry. I didn't mean to startle you."

"What are you doing here already? I said I would call you." She stood next to Roxy, watching the detective and feeling glad to have the dog at her side. "Your car isn't outside, how did you even get here?"

Detective Jaffrey flicked his wrist. "I rented a boat to do some fishing and I want to get my money's worth before I return it tomorrow." He pulled an envelope from his pocket. "Don't you want to read what's in here?"

Annie nodded.

"Well, I need something from you first." He carefully held his arm. "I hurt my arm and I need some antibiotics or something like that. I checked in your bathroom cabinet, but it's empty."

Annie moved closer to him. "Let me see. Roll up your sleeve."

The detective gingerly pushed his sleeve up to reveal a red and pus-filled wound.

Annie touched around the redness. "This is badly infected. Have you thought about going to the emergency room?"

"I hate doctors. Don't you have something?"

"I haven't put all my stuff away yet. It's probably in my backpack still."

She returned with a tube of antibiotic cream. "I don't think this will help much at this point, but here you go."

Detective Jaffrey smeared the cream on the wound and pulled his shirt sleeve down. "Thanks."

Annie watched as Smokey peeked out from under the couch and pounced on Roxy's tail.

"Roy told me that Max hid drugs inside your photographs."

Annie's gaze left the kitten's antics to settle on the detective's face. "Why would my father tell you?"

"Didn't you know?"

Annie checked the time on her watch. "Listen, I need to be somewhere soon so can you please spit out whatever it is you want to tell me?"

He smirked. "I'm working for your father. He hired me to find you."

Annie put two and two together from the information her mother had found in Roy's desk and tried to hide her anger. "How long have you been following me?"

The detective settled onto the couch. "I thought that would get your attention. Oh, I found you right after you left two years ago, but Roy wanted me to keep an eye on you. He wanted to make sure you were safe. And it turns out, you hooked up with some shady people."

"So, you're a private detective?"

"Yeah. Everyone assumed I was working with the police department and I never bothered to correct anyone. I doubt I can keep it up for much longer though, now that your ex fiancé, Tyler, is starting to ask questions about that knife you found at the café."

"Is it the murder weapon?" Annie whispered the question.

"Yeah, it sure is."

"Jake murdered Max?"

"It's his knife. Listen, Annie, I need those drugs, so where are they and I'll get out of your life."

Annie's mind raced. She had to get to the café where there would be more people. "Roy already found them."

"What?" The detective stood up and paced around the room. "He's double crossing me, that piece of scum. He was supposed to find out what you knew since my charm wasn't working on getting any info. 'Get the info and give it to me.' That was his plan." He ran his hands through his hair as he continued to pace.

"What difference does it make? He can just turn it over to the police."

"Sorry to disappoint you, but nothing is getting turned over to the police. Vincent and I worked too hard getting this drug distribution going for everything to end because you decided to run away from your boyfriend."

Understanding began to dawn in Annie's brain. "Was Max involved?" Annie held her breath, not wanting to hear the truth if she had completely misjudged Max.

Detective Jaffrey laughed an evil laugh. "We couldn't get him on board; he was too honest and was always worrying about helping all the poor starving artists."

Annie picked Smokey up and patted her soft fur as she sank down into the cushions of her chair. She wanted to keep Detective Jaffrey talking until she understood what was going on. "If Max wasn't involved, how did the drugs get behind my photos? He did the matting and framing."

"Vincent screwed up. He put it there after Max finished but he didn't know Max was going to come back and put the photographs in your car. He must have figured out what was going on."

"And my father?"

"He wanted to keep you safe. He had the brilliant idea to burn down your aunt's café to get you to go back to Catfish Cove and get you away from the gallery. When you left without telling anyone, taking the photographs and the drugs, you led us all here."

Annie's head was spinning. Roy burned down the café? Her father wanted her to come back? Why didn't he just tell her? She knew it wouldn't have convinced her but he could have tried. "I don't believe this. Are you going to show me that paper?"

Detective Jaffrey remembered the envelope he held in his hand. "Oh, yeah. Here."

Annie held the paper lightly, as if it might burst into flames. It shook in her trembling hands. She searched in the detective's eyes, hoping to see some indication of what might be on the paper before she unfolded it. His cold eyes gave her no clues.

She unfolded the paper and saw a seal from the court of New Hampshire at the top center, not an adoption agency letterhead which was what she was expecting. She read that the record of her birth information was sealed and it was signed by Judge Warren Hunter. "What does this mean?"

"Sorry, it's the dead end that Max came to. Your birth information is not accessible."

She read it again. Judge Hunter? Was he related to her landlord, Jason Hunter? The same judge who got Leona out of jail all those years ago? She would try to track him down with this document and demand an explanation.

Annie looked up at Detective Jaffrey when he stood and stretched and his words broke through her thoughts. "I'm tired of explaining. I want the drugs."

She felt trapped and struggled to keep breathing. "They're at the café."

Detective Jaffrey smacked his head. "I knew it. I should have torn Leona's cafe up from top to bottom instead of just dumping the chili to try to scare the two of you. Let's go. You drive."

"I need a few minutes." Annie hustled around her apartment fixing a bed for Roxy, checking that she was comfortable, and thinking. If she hadn't been so stubborn, she told herself, she would have told Tyler the plan. Now she had to figure out how to stay in control of the situation. Detective Jaffrey wanted something she had so she would dangle it like a carrot.

The detective took Annie's arm before she was ready but he was sick of her stalling tactics. "Let's go."

It only took five minutes to drive to the Cove's Corner building but it felt like an eternity to Annie. From the parking lot, the building appeared to be dark and deserted but as they walked to the entrance off the deck, lights shone through from the café.

His grip on Annie's arm tightened. "Looks like something's going on inside. Are you bringing me into some kind of trap?"

"You said you want the drugs, and this is where they are. You're not the only one after them."

"Alright, but you're staying with me."

Detective Jaffrey walked into the café keeping Annie in front of him. Leona stood behind the counter while Roy, Jake and Vincent argued with each other.

"Why did you bring him?" Roy asked Annie with a scowl on his face.

"He didn't exactly give me a choice. So, Dad, this fine detective you hired thinks you're double crossing him. And it was you who burned Leona's café down?"

Leona's face went white. "You?" She pulled out her cell phone.

Detective Jaffrey twisted Annie's arm behind her back. "Drop your phone Leona, unless you want to hear her scream when I break her arm. Let's not get sidetracked away from the main attraction. Roy, Annie tells me you found something I've been looking for. Hand it over and your little girl here won't get hurt." He pushed Annie's arm higher and she gasped as she stood on her tippy toes to relieve the pressure.

"Hey. I told you. Keep her out of this," Roy sneered.

"Yeah, you told me, but I'm done following your orders. This is my show now. Slide the bag over to me nice and slow."

Roy did as he was told and Detective Jaffrey bent down to pick up the bag. "Great. Don't get any funny ideas about calling the police or anything. Annie's coming with me and I won't hurt her if you all stay calm and quiet." He winked at Leona. "Sorry I can't hang around to get to know you better, sweetheart, but that's life."

Detective Jaffrey pulled Annie out of the café and back to her car. "Get in. I'm driving."

Chapter 23

Annie rubbed some circulation back into her arm as her brain ran through her options. That hadn't gone at all how she'd hoped. Even with Martha and her mother as back up in the Fabric Stash, she never had a chance to give them a warning to call Tyler.

"What's your plan now?" she asked, trying to sound calm.

"Your time is up."

A chill ran through Annie's body. *Those words*. It wasn't the first time they had rung in her ears. Everything clicked together in her brain "You left that message on Max's phone," she managed to whisper through her clenched teeth. "It was you, not Vincent or Jake who killed Max."

Detective Jaffrey pushed on the accelerator.

Annie swung her hand and hit him on his wounded arm. "How does that feel? Max stabbed you with that awl and gave you that nasty puncture wound, didn't he?"

The detective gasped in pain. "Max was a fool. He was so frantic to find you he never considered that Vincent and I would follow him. It was pathetic how Max begged me to just leave town and he would get the drugs back. But he knew too much. He came here to warn you and I couldn't let that happen, now, could I? This pain can't stop me." He reached over and ran his fingers down Annie's cheek. "I heard the lake is nice and deep right out from your apartment and I'll be long gone while they're still looking for you."

Annie's old Saab sputtered and died. For once she smiled at her car instead of cursing. Detective Jaffrey slammed his hands on the steering wheel. "What's the matter with this piece of crap car? It only had to make it back to your apartment and to my boat." He glared at her. "What's wrong with it?"

"Well, Sally's a bit temperamental and she doesn't like anyone to drive but me."

"Sally? You named your car?"

Annie shrugged, hoping this would give her a chance to escape. She only needed one opportunity and every nerve in her body surged, ready to flee.

"Okay, you drive but no funny stuff. Slide over while I go around."

He got out of the car, keeping his eyes on Annie as she slid to the driver side. He scooted around to the passenger door but Annie turned the key and hit the power locks, promising way more than to give up chocolate for life this time if Sally started. She threw in ice cream with hot fudge sauce and crossed her fingers for good luck, too.

Sally started up on the first turn and Annie jammed her foot on the accelerator, knocking the Detective Jaffrey off his feet. She spun the car around, heading back toward the detective who stared frozen with wide eyes as she aimed straight for him.

Blue flashing lights approached from the opposite direction and she slammed on her brakes at the last second, stopping mere inches from the detective. Tyler's police cruiser blocked him in between the cruiser and Annie's Saab.

Detective Jaffrey's head swiveled around, looking for an escape route. He was trapped like a deer caught in headlights. Tyler jumped out of his cruiser and had handcuffs on the detective before Annie even let her breath out. She sat behind the wheel, gripping it to help control her shaking, until her knuckles turned white.

More cars screeched to a stop behind Tyler's cruiser and the first people to get to Annie's car were Mia and Leona. Mia opened the car door and gently uncurled Annie's fingers from the steering wheel, pulling her into her arms. "We were so worried when we saw Detective Jaffrey take you out with him, we decided to call Tyler before we even knew what had happened. Nothing made sense, but we knew there wasn't any time to wait for an explanation."

Annie fell against her mother's shoulder. "I'm so glad you did, Mom. I think he planned to dump me in the lake."

Roy appeared behind Mia. "Annie, I'm so sorry. This was all my fault. I only wanted to protect you but I almost got you killed."

Leona dragged Roy away and Annie whispered to her mom, "I wouldn't want to be dad now, Leona's going to rip him a new you know what!"

Annie pushed away from her mother, running to Tyler. "Don't let Vincent get away. All the drugs are packed in boxes in his car."

Martha huffed and puffed over to Annie. "Oh, hon, you're a welcome sight for these old eyes. You don't have to worry about that Vinny varmint anymore. You should have seen the look on his face when he slipped into the puddle of fish guts next to the dock."

Annie's face relaxed and her mouth turned up into a big grin. "I hope he didn't mess up that shiny suit of his," she said sarcastically.

"Oh, there were just a wee bit of fish scales sticking to his clothes."

"What was he doing by the docks?"

Mia interrupted, "Martha, bless her heart, had the presence of mind to disconnect the battery in his car when he went into the café. We thought he was the murderer, and if his car wouldn't start, he wouldn't get too far, now would he?"

Martha butted in to finish her tale. "It worked like a charm, and when he tried to make a run for it, splat, right into the fish guts. Head first. He's going to stink up that jail cell pretty quickly. Poor Tyler."

They all broke down into a fit of uncontrollable laughter with the image of Vincent covered in smelly fish scales sitting on a cold metal bench in the jail cell next to Detective Jaffrey.

After Tyler put the detective in the back of the cruiser, he asked Annie if she felt good enough to go to the station to give a statement.

She nodded with her hand over her mouth, trying to stop the giggles. Jason suddenly appeared at her side telling Tyler he would bring Annie since she was in no condition to drive. Mia and Leona said they would check on Smokey and Roxy and wait at Annie's apartment for her to get back. Annie watched all the action as if in a slow motion dream.

Jason led her to his car. Max's warning to not trust anyone shrieked in her head. She stopped and looked at Jason. "Can I trust you?"

"Yes."

Staring into his dark eyes, she saw his honesty reflected back to her and she slid into the passenger seat of his car.

Jason asked, "You never suspected Detective Jaffrey did you?"

"Not until I heard his voice tell me 'your time is up.' Those exact words in that evil voice was the message on Max's answering machine before I left. That and his injured arm." She turned her body to face Jason. "There was always something about him but I couldn't put my finger on it until that moment."

Annie gave her statement to Tyler and once they matched the blood on the awl to Detective Jaffrey's blood, there would be another piece of evidence against him.

"Go on home now, Annie. I know where to find you if I have any more questions." He hugged her. "I'm glad we aren't dredging the lake for your body."

"Me too."

Jason pulled into the driveway between her apartment and his house. "I'll walk you to the door, if you don't mind."

She smiled. "Come on in if you want."

"I need to run to my house, but I'll be back."

Roxy was sitting and waiting inside the door for Annie to return. "Hi girl." Roxy gently put her two front paws on Annie's chest and stared into her eyes, searching to be sure Annie was alright.

Leona laughed. "She hasn't left that spot since we got here. She just sat down, staring at the door, waiting for you to walk in."

Jason came back in less than five minutes, carrying a bottle of wine and a frozen eggplant parmesan. "Anyone hungry?"

Leona winked at Annie and whispered as she walked by to take the casserole from Jason, "Don't let this one get away!"

Behind the scenes with Lyndsey

I love picking blueberries at the U-Pick farm down the road from where I live. It's a cleared area with about 300 bushes nestled in the middle of the woods. Last year I brought my two grandsons along to "help". The younger one, Danny, is two so he was happy to sit in front of a bush and pick the low hanging fruit. Needless to say, none of his berries ended up in our containers!

My older grandson, Mark, is four and he chatted and picked happily following along with me. He's at that age where he never runs out of questions: "Mimi, why are some of the berries green? Shouldn't they be called greenberries? Mimi, how many bushes are there?" It went on and on this way until I noticed he was quiet, looking toward the trees at the edge of the field.

"Mimi, you know what my favorite birds are? I like the red cardinals and the blue cardinals best." I saw that he was looking at several blue jays squawking like they always do, and sitting quietly near them was one brilliant red cardinal. The blue jays and cardinals are similar in size and shape so in my grandson's eyes they are all cardinals. For the rest of my life, I will look at the blue jays with this memory of my day picking blueberries and seeing "blue cardinals" for the first time!

After the adventure of picking, the next bit of fun starts. We all work together to make . . .

Blueburied Muffins

First things first, though. Mark and Danny need a snack after all the hard work of picking so I get them set up at my kitchen island with a glass of milk and a Blueburied Muffin that I already have on hand (they store great!). It took me some time to figure out that the kids were the most helpful while eating a snack, giving me time to get most of the batter put together. While they chatter away happily and eat their snack I get all the ingredients out and get started.

First I preheat the oven to 375 F.

In a large bowl I mix together, with an electric mixer for about 2 minutes until light and fluffy:

- ½ cup unsalted butter
- 1 ¼ cups white sugar

Then I add 2 eggs to the butter/sugar mix—one at a time until everything is well blended. I use my own eggs from my backyard chickens which makes it nice and deep yellow.

In another bowl I mix the dry ingredients together:

- 2 cups all purpose flour
- ½ teaspoon salt
- 2 teaspoons baking powder

I measure ½ cup milk into a third container and set it aside.

At this point, the boys are about done with their snack so I save this next job for them.

I try to have some fancy muffin papers just for when they visit and they get the important job of carefully lining the 12 cup muffin pan while I mix everything together.

With the three bowls in front of me, I mix the dry ingredients (flour, salt and baking powder) into the creamed mixture (butter, sugar and eggs) alternately with the ½ cup milk. The process is to add about ½ the dry mixture, then the ½ cup milk, then the rest of the dry mixture. But don't forget to mix after each addition.

By now, Mark and Danny have the muffin pans lined and the last task is ready for them. They get to dump 2 cups of blueberries, lightly dusted with flour, into the batter. That's where they came up with the name Blueburied! All those berries cover the batter and they laugh thinking it's about the funniest thing they've seen. Every time! A few stirs to mix the berries into the batter and it's time to spoon the batter into the muffin cups. Fill each muffin cup about 2/3 full.

The pan can be put into the oven at this point, or, if you like them a little sweeter, you can sprinkle a little sugar on the top of each uncooked muffin. I'm sure you can guess what happens in my house! Yup. Our muffins get that sprinkle of sugar and finally they go into the preheated oven for 25-30 minutes. Sometimes I forget to set the timer but a good test is to check a couple of muffins with a toothpick to make sure they are done. The toothpick should come out clean, unless, of course, you spear a blueberry.

One last thought . . . This recipe is easy to double if you're expecting company, because I know how fast they disappear in my house and I bet they'll go fast in yours too!

Enjoy!

~Lyndsey

ABOUT THE AUTHOR

Lyndsey Cole lives in New England in a small rural town with her husband, dogs, cats and chickens. She has plenty of space to grow lots of beautiful perennials. Sitting in the garden with the scent of lilac, peonies, lily of the valley or whatever is in bloom, stimulates her imagination about mysteries and romance.

ONE LAST THING . . .

If you enjoyed this installment of Lily Bloom Cozy Mystery Series, be sure to join my FREE COZY MYSTERY BOOK CLUB! Be in the know for new releases, promotions, sales, and the possibility to receive advanced reader copies. Join the club here—http://LyndseyColeBooks.com

OTHER BOOKS BY LYNDSEY COLE

<u>Begonias Mean Beware — A Lily Bloom Cozy Mystery</u>

Misty Valley has a new flower shop in town, and as soon as Lily Bloom hangs the open sign, she lands the biggest wedding in town. Plus, the handsome new guy moves in right next door to Lily. She's well on her way to a successful and exciting season.

But when the groom is found dead in her kitchen just days before he's supposed to be walking down the aisle, Lily has to arrange the trail of flowers to try to solve the mystery. With the help of her scooter-riding, pot-smoking mother, Iris, her sister, Daisy, and her dog, Rosie, Lily races from one disaster to another, all the while keeping herself out of the killer's sight.

Will she solve the cascade of events in time or get caught by the criminals running illegal gambling and selling drugs in Misty Valley? Will romance blossom between Lily and her new neighbor?

Queen of Poison – A Lily Bloom Cozy Mystery

Business at Lily's Beautiful Blooms Flower Shop is growing like weeds after a rainstorm. She's been asked to do the main flower arrangement for the Arts in Bloom opening at the Misty Valley Museum. Everything seems to be coming up rosy and she's even falling head over heels for the man of her dreams, Ryan Steele, her neighbor and the police chief of Misty Valley.

Until she sees a sleek red convertible drive into his driveway. And an even sleeker red head climbs out of the car. She thought that was all she had to deal with until the founder of the museum drops dead in her arms and another body has all fingers pointing toward Lily.

With help from her mom, Iris, her sister, Daisy and their friends Marigold and Tamara, Lily tries to arrange the clues to point to the real killer. Can she sort it out in time before a third body—maybe hers—ends up in the morgue? Can she get her romance growing again with the handsome police chief of Misty Valley? Or will she be left to sort through the clues alone?

Roses are Dead – A Lily Bloom Cozy Mystery

Business is popping for Lily as wedding season is in full swing. The brides are all over the place from easy-to-please to last-minute-panics. But one in particular stands out—a leggy brunette who is looking for plenty of red roses for her wedding to Police Chief Ryan Steele.

Lily is beside herself with betrayal that Ryan would lead her on like that, all the while engaged to this beauty. It's almost too much to take until the bride is found dead, surrounded by none other than the very roses she'd been admiring.

Lily shoots to the top of the suspect list, a place she's been all too often lately. And as she starts to uncover more about the woman's past, she's thrown into another game of cat and mouse. Only she's not sure if she's the cat or the mouse. Will she be able to follow the clues to the real killer in time? Or is everyone connected to Ryan Steele in danger and Lily could be next?

Drowning in Dahlias – A Lily Bloom Cozy Mystery

The business is heating up at Beautiful Blooms and Lily's flower arrangements can be found all over Misty Valley at any type of event. And to add to the chaos, she's lost the full time help of her sister, Daisy, who has started a specialty cake making business on the side. Together, they make the perfect team, especially when wealthy estate owner, Walter Nash, enlists both of them to cater and decorate for the 55th birthday party for his wife.

But when they show up with their deliveries and find the love of his life, Harriet Nash, dead on the floor, the dynamic duo is suddenly threatened. With a house full of family and friends to celebrate her birthday, there are too many suspects to keep straight.

Lily's biggest challenge now is to find the killer before the killer finds her. But without a murder weapon at the crime scene, the questions continue to pile up without any answers. Who would have wanted Harriet dead the most? She had plenty of money, but would someone have been so greedy? As Lily and Daisy get closer to solving the murder, things take a turn for the worse with a threat on Lily's life.

Hidden by the Hydrangeas – A Lily Bloom Cozy Mystery

Lily Bloom can't seem to keep her thoughts away from marriage. Maybe it's just because her mom tied the knot with her childhood sweetheart Walter Nash, but it's gotten Lily thinking about her own relationship with Ryan Steele and if it's going anywhere.

But those thoughts are quickly replaced with who is carrying a dead body, and who that dead body might be. The only thing Lily knows is that she's been spotted by the killer so she has to hope this mystery is solved before she's the next one in a body bag.

When Walter's best friend turns up as the likeliest suspect, Lily's mom is beside herself with worry and convinces Lily that she's the best person to solve this case. But suspects keep piling up with not quite enough evidence to prove anything. Will Lily be able to put all the pieces together before the killer sniffs out her trail?

Christmas Tree Catastrophe – A Lily Bloom Cozy Mystery

Lily Bloom couldn't be more excited for Christmas Eve when she will say "I do" to the man she loves. She just has the library opening to get through and then all the town's focus will be on her.

But things start going wrong almost from the very first moment she's getting setup for the library's event. Not only is there plenty of disagreement among those helping, but one of the co-chairs who is in charge of the whole event winds up dead the day before the ceremony.

With everyone who was helping setup under a microscope, Lily is in a race against time to be able to get married. When one of her best friends winds up in jail for the murder Lily knows she didn't commit, the pressure's on to find the real murderer.

Will Lily be able to prove her friend's innocence? Or will she find herself in even more trouble and face a wedding in a jail cell or the hospital? Or worse—will there be no wedding at all because the bride is the new target?

Made in the USA
Lexington, KY
30 December 2016